Be long. You'll fall in love. You'll want to marry him and have his children. Why are you—"

"It's not necessary that you understand," she interrupted, erasing all emotion from her voice. "I won't be getting married. I won't be having anyone else's children. Trust me on that."

Ben was taken aback by the cool formality of her words.

"I do," he said, caught in a moment of involuntary candor. "I don't believe there's a man alive who could melt your icy heart."

He watched her chin tip upward, her mouth tighten.

"You're absolutely right," she said. "Now, do we have a deal or not?"

Dear Reader,

This month, our FABULOUS FATHER starts off
Linda Varner's exciting new series, MR. RIGHT, INC.
The trilogy features three pals who find love at first site—
construction site that is. Ethan Cooper is a *Dad on the Job.*
He wasn't looking for love—just a good life for him and his
kids. Then he met Nicole Winter....

Favorite author Marie Ferrarella continues her BABY'S
CHOICE series with *Baby Times Two.* In this heartwarming
series, matchmaking babies bring together their unsuspecting
parents—and inspire them to love.

Silhouette Romance is proud to present the newest star to
the line, Christie Clark. Her book, *Two Hearts Too Late,* is
our PREMIERE title. We know you'll be pleased with this
emotional story of two people who fall in love—in the midst
of a custody battle.

Wedding bells are ringing for two of our couples this month.
Watch Kristi Beeler turn handsome cynic Matt Stewart into
a dashing groom in Maris Soule's *Stop the Wedding!* And
Ben Danvers and Chelsea Carson strike a marriage bargain
in Donna Clayton's latest book, *Wife for a While.*

What happens when a handsome ghost hunter and a beautiful
skeptic join forces to investigate the strange happenings in an
old house? Find out in *Turn Back the Night* by Jennifer Drew—
an exciting SPELLBOUND title.

I hope you've enjoyed Silhouette Romance this month.
In the coming months look for books by Elizabeth August,
Helen R. Myers, Joleen Daniels, Carla Cassidy and
many more of your favorite authors!

Happy reading!

Anne Canadeo
Senior Editor

Please address questions and book requests to:
Silhouette Reader Service
U.S.: 3010 Walden Ave., P.O. Box 1325, Buffalo, NY 14269
Canadian: P.O. Box 609, Fort Erie, Ont. L2A 5X3

WIFE FOR A WHILE

Donna Clayton

Silhouette
R O M A N C E™
Published by Silhouette Books
America's Publisher of Contemporary Romance

For Judy and Colleen—
true friends.
My thanks to Evan Milburn of Milburn's Orchard, Elkton,
Maryland, who patiently answered a million and one
questions. And to Janice Potts, Deputy Clerk of the Cecil
County Court, Marriage Bureau, Elkton, Maryland,
who hears "I will" every day.

 SILHOUETTE BOOKS

ISBN 0-373-19039-5

WIFE FOR A WHILE

Books by Donna Clayton

Silhouette Romance

Mountain Laurel #720
Taking Love in Stride #781
Return of the Runaway Bride #999
Wife for a While #1039

DONNA CLAYTON

Having my first manuscript acknowledged by Romance Writers of America as a Golden Heart Finalist Award winner was a joy for me. When Silhouette bought the manuscript and published *Mountain Laurel,* I felt my dream had come true. Now, several books later, my excitement over creating new characters not only lingers…it continues to grow! My deep love of reading has turned into a successful career in writing.

Every writer puts a little piece of herself in every book she writes, in every character she brings to life. Each novel I have written holds a special place in my heart. *Wife for a While* is especially cherished. Not only is this the most sensuous book I have written, but the story also deals with a serious social issue.

Child abuse comes in many forms—physical, psychological, sexual, neglect. If you, like my heroine, are a survivor of child abuse, start the healing process now. A counselor is available to help you twenty-four hours a day. Call Childhelp/IOF Foresters National Child Abuse Hotline at 1-800-4-A-CHILD. (If you are hearing impaired and have TDD, call 1-800-2-A-CHILD.)

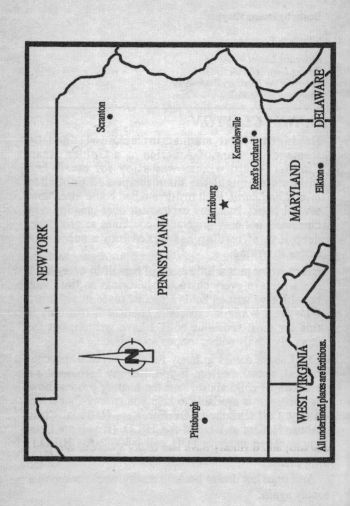

NEW YORK

PENNSYLVANIA

Scranton •

Kemblesville •
Reed's Orchard •

Harrisburg ★

Pittsburgh •

WEST VIRGINIA

MARYLAND

Elkton •

DELAWARE

All underlined places are fictitious.

N

Chapter One

Today's the day, Chelsea Carson thought, and although the rare smile that tilted her eyes widened a fraction, she couldn't deny the fierce anxiety that knotted in her stomach. Unwittingly, she pressed a quelling palm against her abdomen.

"I will do it," she said aloud. "I will."

But her determined voice was lost on the cool spring breeze that blew through the apple orchard.

For nearly two weeks she'd worked at gathering the inner strength, the sheer guts it would take to make the offer, an offer that wasn't entirely unselfish. Chelsea was certain she could do it. She had to. Because when she did, she'd finally have her heart's desire, her life-long dream.

And once her dream became reality, she'd never feel lonely again.

Loneliness. Lately it had engulfed her, nearly smothered her. Oh, it wasn't as though she were alone. She came into contact with people every day in her job as the bookkeeper and office manager here at Reed's Orchard. In fact, she could think only of a few times in her life when she hadn't been surrounded by people. It was just that she'd learned firsthand how dangerous it was to become too friendly with those around her.

Yes, Chelsea had found it necessary to hold herself apart, and because of this necessity she'd often been labeled as cool, even aloof. But she didn't mind. These character traits were her armor, and they were essential for her survival.

But if her plan was successful, the loneliness that had plagued her for so long would be a thing of the past, a distant, unpleasant memory—an unpleasant memory she would place on the shelf in the back of her mind with all the others.

In order for her plan to come to fruition, however, Chelsea knew she must—

"Be bold," she whispered, rounding the corner of the brick building that housed the orchard's offices and produce market. "March right up to him and say..."

The thought died mid-stream at the sight of Ben Danvers. He stood with his back to her at the opposite end of the small asphalt parking lot—feet planted apart, arms crossed at his chest—obviously embroiled in a confrontation with the potbellied, balding man in front of him.

"Take it down."

Chelsea overheard Ben's demand, a demand made in a dangerously calm tone.

"But the auction's next week," the man protested. "That sign serves as advertisement. People will come in droves to buy up this land, if you'll only—"

Ben stepped over to the newly planted sign promoting the auctioning of Reed's Orchard. Placing his shoulder beneath the rectangle of plywood, Ben rocked the post several times and hauled the whole works from the ground.

"Wait!" the fat man shouted. "Stop! I just—"

Ben threw the sign at the auctioneer's feet.

"This land still belongs to me," Ben informed him.

"But—" the fat man's face reddened in anger "—only until next week."

Ben's voice remained deadly calm as he stated, "You will not put that sign on my land."

The large man huffed and puffed as he dragged the sign to the back of his truck and hefted it into the bed of the pickup. He grumbled under his breath as he climbed behind the steering wheel and threw a glare at Ben. "I'll be back. Don't you worry."

Chelsea watched the auctioneer drive away with a squeal of tires. Then her gaze riveted on the stiff posture of Ben's back. He was in deep trouble, she knew. His time was running out.

I can help him. The thought made nerves dance in her stomach like the flapping wings of a thousand butterflies.

He can help me. The selfish words came unbidden to her mind. A pang of guilt sliced through her heart and forced her gaze to slide to the ground.

With great effort, Chelsea lifted her chin and straightened her shoulders. "I will do this," she whispered determinedly. "For once in your life, Chelsea, be bold."

Pushing open the door, she disappeared into the brick building.

Agitated, Ben raked his fingers through his already disheveled hair. He turned and stomped across the parking lot, heaving a tremendous sigh. He had to do something to save his orchard—and he had to do it quickly. But what was he supposed to do? Pluck a woman out of midair? Grab some unknown female off the street and haul her to the altar?

Entering the country store, Ben saw Aunt May sitting behind the counter reading one of her coveted tabloid newspapers.

May glanced up, her eyes twinkling with excitement. "There's this little waitress in Mississippi who says she's been abducted by aliens forty times over the past eighteen months."

Usually, May's outlandish stories would give Ben a good chuckle, but today he didn't even smile. It was obvious she saw his distress, because she folded the paper and tucked it underneath the counter.

"Why did he do it, May?" Ben could hear his growing frustration leaking into his question, but he couldn't help it. He was just about at the end of his rope.

"The auctioneer was only trying to do his job," Aunt May explained gently.

Ben shook his head. "I'm not talking about the auctioneer. I mean Granddad. Why is he taking all this—" he lifted his hands in a grand, sweeping motion "—away from me?"

"It wasn't his intention to hurt you." May's voice was hushed, almost a whisper.

"Aunt May, he not only hurt me, he cheated me." His voice had a matter-of-fact quality to it.

"Oh, Ben." The two little words held all the sympathy and compassion she was feeling. "I don't know what he was thinking. John Reed was my brother, but for the life of me I never could quite figure him out."

"Forced marriage." Ben's tone was just as incredulous now as it had been over two weeks ago at the reading of his grandfather's will. "This hasn't been done for a hundred years."

May could only give an empathic nod.

"If I don't comply with that clause—" Ben rubbed at the tension building in the muscles at the back of his neck "—if I don't get married by next week, my orchard is going to be auctioned off." He pointed vaguely toward the door. "That pack of apathetic lawyers in town is going to sell my land to the highest bidder and give the profits to a list of charities that's as long as my arm."

Ben knew it was unfair of him to blame the lawyers who were handling his grandfather's estate—hell, he didn't even know them. But the need to lash out was strong, and at the moment Ben didn't care to deny it.

Pressing her lips together, May looked as though she couldn't think of a proper response.

"This land has been in our family for five genera-
tions." Stress fueled Ben's frustration. "And now that
it's time for the orchard to be passed on to me, I'm
going to lose it all. All because of a willful, old coot!"

May's spine straightened. "I want to remind you
that that willful, old coot was your grandfather. I
won't have you talking about him that way. You were
just a baby when your father died, and your grandfather saw to it that you and your mother were taken
care of. And then after your mother passed away, he
raised you the best he could—"

"I know. I know, Aunt May," Ben relented. "I owe
you and Granddad everything. I do know that." He
planted one fist on his hip. "But why this?" he asked.
"Why force me to get married?"

May shrugged. "Maybe John wanted you to have
someone you could share all this with. Maybe he
wanted you to have a wife and children of your own—
so you could experience the same happiness he'd
found with your grandmother and your mother."

Ben thrust his hands up into the air, his eyes im-
ploring. "But why the time frame of twenty-one days?
I had no objection to marriage. I would have settled
down one day. Eventually, I would have found myself
a wife and had a few kids." He shook his head and
sighed. "But all that takes time. And I've been
spending all of mine building up Reed's Orchard."

"Maybe your grandfather noticed that, too," May
commented.

A disgusted sound burst from the back of Ben's
throat. "But May, how am I supposed to woo a
woman to the altar in such a short time?"

"Time's getting shorter every day," May reminded him pointedly.

"This situation is impossible, I'm telling you." Ben ran a hand over his jaw. His tone lowered as though he were speaking to himself as he asked, "What could Granddad have been thinking?"

May rested her elbows on the counter and leaned forward. "John was a loving and caring man. He provided for his family. He went to church regularly. He was an upstanding citizen." She tucked a wispy strand of gray hair back into place atop her tightly teased beehive hairdo. "But I must admit that at times he could get some quirky notions into his head."

A small chuckle rumbled in her ample chest before she continued. "Remember the time . . . you were just a boy . . . when your grandfather found that clay pot shard on a plot of ground he bought off Duck Neck Road?"

Although Ben knew the place his aunt spoke of— there was a well-developed grove of apple trees there now—he shook his head, unable to recall the particular incident.

May couldn't contain her grin. "Well, John was certain he'd come upon a great archaeological find. He contacted the community college, but they weren't interested. So he called some of the universities in Philadelphia. Two professors came out to have a look-see, but in the end they told John it was nothing—that he should just go ahead and plant his trees." May leaned back, resting her chubby forearm on the arm of the chair. "John wouldn't listen to the experts, though. He decided to excavate himself. He didn't know a thing about digging up ancient relics, but he dug just the same.''

''What did he find?'' Ben asked.

''Dirt.''

Ben was helpless against the smile that curled the corners of his mouth. ''I do remember when he lost all that money.''

May laughed at the memory she, too, obviously remembered well.

''He'd had a dream,'' Ben said. ''Granddad was certain he knew the winning lottery numbers—he was going to be a millionaire. He played a hundred dollars a day for nearly a month before he gave up.''

''And that stubborn man never did admit defeat,'' May added. ''He simply grumbled about the whole setup being fixed. Of course it wasn't fixed.''

There was a moment of silence as both Ben and May thought about some of John Reed's other odd exploits. Ben had loved his grandfather dearly, but he did have to admit that there were times when the man was slightly off kilter. And this forced-marriage deal was simply another one of those times.

''Like I said,'' May finally commented, ''sometimes John got some quirky notions into his head. But don't go thinking you can fight the will. Having John Reed declared incompetent would be impossible, because he was as sane as Solomon.'' She hooted before she added, ''Too bad he wasn't as wise.''

''My lawyer agrees with you,'' Ben said. ''About fighting the will, I mean. He says there are too many people here in Kemblesville who would testify to Granddad's 'soundness of mind.' Besides, the legal fees alone would force me to mortgage the orchard, or worse, sell it. So I don't see how I can win in this situation." He inhaled deeply. "I really don't believe Granddad was incompetent. If he had been, he couldn't have kept Reed's Orchard going all those years. I guess he was just . . ." His voice trailed off as he searched for the correct adjective to describe John Reed.

"Quirky?" May provided.

Ben closed his eyes and nodded.

He perched his hip on the counter, hung his head and rubbed the knuckle of his index finger back and forth across his bottom lip in contemplation. Finally, he said, "Well, Granddad's eccentricity is sure to ruin me this time. I can't for the life of me think of a way out of this one."

"Looks pretty cut and dried to me," May said, her tone blunt and to the point. "You need to find a wife."

"That's easy for you to say." He lowered his hand to his thigh, swiping several times at an imaginary piece of lint on the soft cotton of his khaki work trousers. "You're not the one who has to approach some unsuspecting woman and ask her to pledge herself to me." After a moment, he added, "For better or for worse."

"Well, I think you need to start doing some approaching," May said.

"I know, I know. I've been thinking about it."

She pursed her lips. "Action is what's called for here, not thinking."

The stress from the looming time constraint put an involuntary shortness in his tone as he answered, "I'll do something."

Immediately, Ben was flooded with a sense of remorse. He had no business taking his frustration out on his great aunt. Her suggestions were only meant to help him—were only offered out of her concern for him—he realized that.

"I'm sorry, Aunt May," he said. He watched her eyes soften.

"I know it's not easy," she said. "If you don't mind my asking, what *do* you plan on doing?" Then, she grinned impishly. "Or rather, *who* do you plan on asking?"

He slid his weight back until he was sitting on the wooden counter and then he rested his arm on top of the cash register. "As a matter of fact," he said, "I have a couple of ideas about who—"

He stopped short when he heard the hinges of the side door leading to the offices squeak open.

"Excuse me."

Ben's gut tightened at the sight of Chelsea Carson, but he was pleased when it was his only reaction. There had been a time when he would have turned beet red and would not have been able to look her in the eye. However, years had passed since he'd made such a fool of himself in front of her, and over the course of those years the acute embarrassment he felt when he came face-to-face with Chelsea had ebbed to a fleeting tinge of chagrin.

"Hi, Chelsea," May called.

Ben watched Chelsea's mouth pull into what he'd describe as a "near smile"—the only kind she had ever displayed in his presence—and she nodded a cordial greeting toward May.

"Trouble with the accounts?" he asked.

"Oh, no," she said. "The books are in perfect order."

He would have been surprised if she'd said anything else—Chelsea was a whiz at bookkeeping. Ben remembered plenty of times when his grandfather touted her as his "right hand" when it came to keeping the accounts. If Chelsea chose to be withdrawn—sometimes she was downright standoffish—around him, then that was her prerogative. She did her job and did it well, and Ben realized he had no right to ask for more than that.

"Could I see you in my office?" She gestured over her shoulder with a pointing thumb.

His brow raised quizzically as he wondered what Chelsea wanted to speak to him about. She'd never sought him out before, but then she'd always gone over the books with Granddad. Now that the old man had passed away, however, Ben thought that maybe it was only natural for her to seek him out. But there was something in her tension-rigid shoulders and the anxiety in her eyes that warned him that another dilemma was about to be revealed.

"I'll be there right away," he told her. He heard the weariness in his voice and it aggravated him. "Right away," he repeated, this time with a bit more fortitude.

She backed through the door, its hinges creaking. He didn't have room on his shoulders to take on another problem. But as sole owner and operator of Reed's Orchard—even if it was only until next week—solving problems was his responsibility.

As he slid off the counter, he cast a questioning glance at May, hoping she could shed some light on what Chelsea's concern might be. May disclaimed any knowledge with a silent shrug.

Pushing through the door, he paused in the tiny hallway outside Chelsea's office. Ever since he'd returned from college years ago, Ben had been in charge of the actual orchard—planting, pruning, harvesting, storing and a million and one other tasks. John Reed had handled both the accounting and the retail-sales end of the business. Now, Ben was liable for the whole shebang. He'd have to get used to the fact that he'd have more dealings with Chelsea now that his grandfather was no longer around to handle the office matters.

She'd always succeeded in conducting herself with cool professionalism. And if she could do it, then so could he. At that moment, Ben realized he would have to look beyond the bad memory of his past behavior toward her—it had only been one incident—and try to form some type of working relationship with the woman.

Chelsea paced the small confines of her office and fought the panic that welled up like a ready-to-erupt geyser.

"Please, Chelsea," she whispered to herself. "Please have the courage to do this. Just this once."

She sat in her chair, picked up a pencil, tapped it once, twice, three times, then dropped it on the desk top, stood and resumed her pacing.

"I will do this. I will."

The knock on her office door made her jump.

"Come in," she called.

Ben stepped inside, leaving the door ajar.

"Hi," he said. "What's up?"

Ben hated the stiffness that never failed to be present when he encountered Chelsea. He had learned long ago to forgo exchanging informal pleasantries with her. Normally, when he met someone he would inquire about the person's health or some other mundane aspect of life, but Chelsea only froze up when asked those questions. Her eyes would turn stony, her tone cautious. It was almost as though she resented his concern, or maybe she simply didn't feel comfortable revealing the answers to him. Whatever the reasons for her behavior, he'd taken to getting straight down to business when he dealt with Chelsea.

He watched the delicate muscles of her throat constrict under the creamy skin of her neck as she swallowed.

"Sit down, Ben," she told him.

He heard a tightness in her voice and wondered if it was the impending problem she was about to expose or simply his presence that made her so obviously uneasy.

She had taken a seat behind the desk and he noticed how she balanced on the very edge of the chair, her back rod-straight. But then he nearly smiled when he realized he was sitting as if on tenterhooks himself. He made a conscious effort to relax back against the chair.

"So, Chelsea," he said. "What's wrong? There's evidently a problem. Whatever it is, we can work it out."

Chelsea inhaled a shaky breath. She wished she had only a modicum of Ben's self-assuredness. She had promised herself she would do this. It was now or never.

"Ben," she began cautiously, "I couldn't help but overhear your conversation with May just now. And I do have to admit it's not the first discussion between the two of you that I've overheard lately." She quickly explained, "It's not that I meant to listen, mind you, it's just that the shop is so close to my office and..."

He nodded and the look in his eyes told her he wasn't offended. She sighed with relief and took a quick moment to form the words in her head for the next sentence she wanted to say.

"I know you're in trouble...with the will and all." Her words were jerky and uneven. "I know you might lose the orchard...and I..." Her voice trailed off as she swallowed.

Ben raised his hand and touched his fingertips to his temple. "Where has my mind been?" It was plain to Chelsea that his question was self-reprimanding.

He stood, took two steps toward the door and then turned back to face her.

"I was so caught up in my own troubles, it never dawned on me that I should have been talking to my employees." Ben came closer to her desk. "You must be wondering if your job is in jeopardy."

"Well, actually—"

"With what's going on," he continued, "I can't tell you that your job is safe. Everything is still so uncertain..." He shook his head. "I can't guarantee anyone's job right now."

Chelsea's felt her brow crease, he looked so remorseful—as though he truly felt he'd somehow let down the people in his employ. Suddenly, some soft, unfamiliar emotion crept through her. It was almost akin to the pity she felt for the wounded animals she cared for at the wildlife reserve where she volunteered her time. But, no, it went deeper than that, it was more like...

Chewing on her bottom lip, she quietly but firmly closed the door on the emotion. *Don't let yourself become involved*, she silently warned herself. That was her number one rule of life. For if she did, invariably she would be hurt.

She was simply going to offer him a deal. She would help him, if he would help her. It was as plain as that.

"Well, actually," she began, "what I wanted to talk to you about has nothing to do with my job."

"Oh?"

Ben's sandy-colored eyebrows raised with his question, and she noticed how they were a shade darker than his hair, which had been bleached by the sun to the color of ripe wheat. Would his hair feel as silky under her fingertips as it looked?

She refused to give the physical awareness a moment's thought. She simply shook her head to clear her mind and continued. "Well, actually," she said, immediately realizing she'd said the phrase a number of times, "it has to do with your problem. You know, the trouble you're in. I think I might have an answer for you.... I might have a plan that could help you.... I mean, I think that—"

Chelsea stopped abruptly. She cleared her throat and took a deep breath. Why wouldn't the words come?

The expression on Ben's face took on a mixture of query, uncertainty and interest, but it was the interest that made his green eyes glitter brightly. She watched him slowly lower himself into the chair opposite her desk.

"Go on," he urged.

When she didn't instantly explain herself, he added, "I don't know what you have in mind, but at this point I'll consider anything." He settled back in the chair, his hands resting on the chair arms, and silently waited.

"Well—" She pressed her lips together, refusing to repeat the word "actually." Her gaze dropped to the pencil resting on her desk and she picked it up. "I know about the clause in your grandfather's will."

She absently fingered the pencil. "I know that if you don't get married, you'll lose the orchard."

The pencil spun between her index finger and thumb. "I know the man from the auction house is anxious to sell. And I know the charities are just as anxious to receive their bequests."

Chelsea took a moment to inhale. At this point the pencil was twirling so quickly that it flew from her fingers and clattered to the floor. Neither she nor Ben moved to touch it.

"Between overhearing your conversation with May," she said, "and hearing odd bits of gossip from various employees, I think I know enough about your situation to know that . . . you need some help."

She saw his eyes narrow with acute attention.

"I think—" she swallowed "—I might be able to help you."

There, she thought, *it's out. Finally.*

Her gaze locked onto Ben as she waited for his response. None came.

"What I mean is," she explained further, "I'm . . . willing to help."

Ben didn't bat an eye. Finally, he shook his head and said, "Help? Chelsea, what exactly is it you're trying to say?"

What was wrong with him? Hadn't he heard her? Didn't he understand her meaning?

As though reading her thoughts, he remarked, "Why don't you tell me the idea you have in mind."

Heat flooded her face. Was he really going to force her to spell it out? Apparently so.

"Well," she began. She looked off over his shoulder. "You're in need of a wife." Lowering her gaze to a spot directly in front of her on the desk, she saw that she was wringing her hands. "I'm . . . single . . . and female."

His green eyes darkened with revelation. "Let me get this straight," he said. "Are you offering to marry me?"

"Well, actually . . . yes."

There was a clatter outside the office door and Ben turned his head.

"Why don't you come on in, Aunt May," he called. "You'll be able to hear much better if you're inside the room rather than standing out in the hallway."

The older lady pushed open the door and then promptly plunked her fists on her broad hips. "Ben Danvers, are you insinuating that I was eavesdropping?" The question held more than a fair measure of indignation.

Ben grinned. "Well, isn't that exactly what you were doing?"

"I was not," May pronounced emphatically. "I was just passin' by the door on my way—" she looked at a momentary loss "—to somewhere important." May changed the subject completely by focusing her boisterous attention on Chelsea. "This is just wonderful! Ben found a wife." She snickered. "Or rather one found him. But is there still time? I'm afraid the registering and blood tests will take too long."

"Now, just slow down, May," Ben said. "Chelsea and I haven't even had a chance to talk about this."

May ignored Ben completely. "I know!" She nearly got her plump body off the ground as she jumped with excitement. "You two can drive into Maryland. The Cecil County courthouse is just over the state line, in Elkton. That little town used to be called the wedding capital of the world, 'cause a couple could get married in two hours." She took a breath and rushed on. "Of course all that's changed now, but I think it only takes two days after registering and you two could be saying 'I do' before the week's out."

"May, please," Ben pleaded. "Let me talk to Chelsea."

Ushering his great aunt out into the hallway, Ben nodded a farewell, stepped back into Chelsea's office and firmly closed the door. He chuckled silently at May's muffled but indignant *harumph*.

"Now," Ben said. "Where were we? I think you had just offered to marry me."

"Of course there would be stipulations," Chelsea was quick to say.

"Of course," Ben said. He felt so overwhelmed by Chelsea's proposition that he welcomed the chance to sit quietly for a moment and listen to the conditions of the arrangement she had in mind.

"There must be a time limit to the union," she said, her tone cool and professional. "We could stay married for say...six months. You'll probably be required to send a copy of our marriage certificate to the lawyers and there may be some other legalities involved." Her head tilted to one side as she said, "But six months should be long enough to take care of any legal aspects that might arise, don't you think?"

Ben could only nod vaguely. He watched her nibble on her full lower lip.

"You're willing to marry me just like that?" he asked. "With no strings attached? I don't get it." He was helpless against the bewilderment in his tone.

"Well, actually...there are some strings attached."

Suspicion rose up around him and made his insides coil like a snake.

"What is it you want, Chelsea? What do you expect to get out of this marriage?"

As he waited for the answers to his questions, Ben wondered just how much money this was going to cost him. Or worse yet, what if she wanted part ownership of the orchard itself? He held his breath, all the while his gut wrenched tighter and tighter.

Chelsea looked at Ben and saw doubt and distrust written all over him; in his expressive green eyes, in the set of his smooth-shaven jaw, in his rigid shoulders and back, in his tightly clenched fists.

This is your chance, she told herself. All the dreams you've ever dreamed can come true—all the hopes you've ever had can be fulfilled—if you handle this right.

Closing her eyes, she gathered every bit of inner strength she had. She inhaled slowly and deeply. Finally, she looked Ben directly in the eye and tipped up her chin.

"I want a baby."

Chapter Two

Ben sat for a moment, stunned to the point of speechlessness. He hadn't heard right. He simply couldn't have heard her correctly.

There were so many things she could have asked for. A lump sum of money. A partnership in the business. The deed to the small house that she lives in rent-free as part of her compensation.

But he'd never have guessed that she wanted a...that she wanted him to... No, he simply hadn't heard her correctly.

Someone asking for what she was asking—from a casual acquaintance, no less—should be a nervous wreck, a babbling idiot or a tongue-tied rattlebrain. Chelsea was none of these things. She looked icy calm, utterly composed. No, he simply hadn't heard correctly... Before he could ask, however, she slowly and succinctly repeated her demand.

"I want a baby."

Chelsea kept her spine stiff, afraid to move a muscle. If he didn't speak soon, she felt she would literally explode. It was obvious that she'd completely dumbfounded him.

"I..." he began. Then he pressed his lips together, his green gaze shifting toward the ceiling and then back to her. "I don't know what to say."

"I have everything all figured out," she said. She knew she must explain her idea in a clear, straightforward manner. Otherwise, he wouldn't understand—or worse, he'd misunderstand—and she'd lose her only chance of having her dream.

A baby. Lord, she wanted a baby so badly she could... but she had to keep her mind on the task of explaining herself to Ben.

Inhaling deeply, she continued, "As I said, I have everything worked out. I'll marry you, thereby fulfilling the terms of your grandfather's will. Reed's Orchard will belong to you. And there will be no more threat of the business being sold."

Her shy gaze lowered to the desk top. "I think we should move in together. That way, making the ... baby ... will be a little easier." The intimate images that thought brought to mind made her whole body grow warm with embarrassment. Closing her eyes, she took a few seconds to compose herself before plowing forward. "I suggest I move in with you," she said, her gaze still glued to the blotter on her desk. "Simply because your house is bigger, and it will mean less of an upset for you."

She took a deep breath, and noticing that her hands had begun to shake, she tucked them in her lap.

"As I said before, I'll remain your wife until all the legal aspects of the will are straightened out." She looked at him and tried to smile. "Oh, and while I'm living with you, I do need to become—" her face flamed and she averted her eyes "—well, you know. The six-month time frame I mentioned before should give us plenty of time to solve both our problems."

"Six months," Ben said, evidently having found his tongue. "What if there are problems?"

"Problems?"

"What if you don't become...well, you know... within the six-month time limit?" he asked. "It's been known to happen."

"I'd be willing to extend the marriage to a year," she said, then quickly added, "in that case."

"Well, what if all those charities that stand to benefit from the sale of Reed's Orchard see this marriage as just what is it?" Ben propped one ankle on his other knee. "A desperate attempt on my part to keep my business. What if they band together, hire a bunch of lawyers and sue? The case could have a life span of—" he exhaled derisively "—years." His gaze locked with hers. "What then?"

She couldn't read the message behind his words. Was he mocking her? Making fun of her? Or simply stating an honest fear? She couldn't tell.

"The clause in your grandfather's will didn't stipulate that you had to marry for love." She was helpless against the sarcastic tone in which she'd stated the final word of her comment. "It's no one's business why we're getting married."

Chelsea straightened in her seat. "Anyway, maybe you're looking for trouble where no trouble exists. I really don't feel there will be any questions asked."

She rubbed her hands over the soft, worn fabric of her jeans. "There are other more important aspects of this that I think you should question. Such as your obligation to this baby as its father. And...the inheritance angle."

Watching his eyebrows jump, she knew she'd gotten his attention.

"Don't worry," she assured him quietly. "I've thought it all out. I don't expect anything from you, Ben. Well," she stumbled over her next thought, "except for the initial...act of...well...you know." She felt her cheeks flood with color and hated herself for the reaction. "What I mean is, you'll father this baby but...you won't be its father. In fact, if everything goes as I've planned, I won't even be here when the baby is born."

"What do you mean?" he asked. "Where will you be?"

"I've lived extremely frugally over the years. I've some money saved. Enough to set me and the baby up somewhere else."

"So, you'll be leaving?"

She licked her lips. "Certainly not until I know for sure that your ownership of the orchard is no longer in question."

Chelsea had meant for the statement to be an assurance, but Ben didn't look the least assured.

"And what about 'the inheritance angle,' as you so casually put it?" he asked.

"I don't want anything that belongs to you. I'll sign anything your lawyer draws up." She swallowed. "But I'll have to ask that you do the same."

"Oh?"

"Yes," she said. "I'll want you to sign over all parental rights."

Chelsea felt pierced by those sharp green eyes as they narrowed on her. She tolerated his stare for as long as she could before dipping her head.

Why was he dragging his feet? she wondered. What was his hesitation? You'd think she was asking for the world. Chelsea's stomach tightened painfully as she discovered she *was* asking for the world—her world. And she wouldn't give up easily.

She looked him directly in the eye. "Ben, I'm not trying to trap you. I'm only trying to offer you a deal. You'll have your orchard and I'll have my baby."

The last few words sounded strangled with suppressed emotion, and Chelsea clamped her lips together when she saw him frown.

You've spoiled everything, she silently railed at herself. She knew very well that when she showed emotion—and she'd certainly raised the curtain on her desperation just now—that the only consequence was hurt and humiliation, for her.

"You certainly have planned this well," he observed, his tone bordering somewhere between anger and sarcasm.

"Look, Ben," she said coolly. "I'm only offering you a solution to your problem. You can't fault me for wanting something for my trouble."

"Something for your trouble? I can't believe some of the things you're saying." He stood up, paced to the door and turned back to face her. "We're talking about a baby here, Chelsea. We're talking about a human life. We're not swapping baseball cards."

Chelsea swallowed around the nervous tension constricting her throat. "I know what we're talking about. Don't you think I've thought long and hard about this?" Her tongue darted out to moisten her dry lips again. "I know exactly what I'm asking. The question is, do you want to keep Reed's Orchard or not? Do you want this deal or not?"

His strong tanned hands clasped the back of the chair he'd been sitting in. When he finally spoke, his voice revealed the terrific amount of bewilderment he was evidently feeling.

"I really don't understand this. Chelsea, you're a young woman. You can't be more than twenty-five or twenty-six—"

"Twenty-eight," she corrected him.

"Nevertheless, you're still a young woman," he said. "You'll be meeting a man before too long. You'll fall in love. You'll want to marry him and have his children. Why are you—"

"It's not necessary that you understand," she interrupted, erasing all emotion from her voice. "I won't be getting married. I won't be having anyone else's children. Trust me on that."

Ben was taken aback by the cool formality of her words.

"I do," he said, caught in a moment of involuntary candor. "I don't believe there's a man alive who could melt your icy heart."

He watched her chin tip upward, her mouth tighten.

"You're absolutely right," she said. "Now, do we have a deal or not?"

Ben felt his fingers digging into the soft upholstery of the chair's back. "It doesn't look as though I have a choice."

Chelsea let herself into the nature center and headed toward the back room where the caged animals were housed. The building had once been a large, rambling barn that had been converted into several spacious rooms used to inform the public about area wildlife.

She stopped at the first metal cage. "Hello, there," she said, her tone quiet, calming.

The shy squirrel skittered behind the tree limb, its tiny nose wiggling furiously as it sniffed the air. The animal had been brought in three days ago. Mauled by a dog, there wasn't much left of the squirrel's bushy tail, but its hind leg looked as though it was mending well. Soon, it would be taken into the woods surrounding the center and released.

Moving slowly so as not to frighten the animal, Chelsea removed the glass water bottle from the side of the cage. She pulled out the rubber stopper, refilled it at the sink and recapped it. She hung the bottle of fresh water back on the cage, so the metal tube was sticking through the bars where the squirrel could reach it.

She unlatched the door to the cage and filled the small plastic feeding dish with a scoop of animal feed, a mixture of nutritious bits mixed with nuts and dried berries.

Chelsea had discovered the center several years ago. She'd found walking the nature paths to be peaceful; the fresh air and tranquillity of the woodland had quickly become an addiction for her.

Offering a few hours of volunteer work had been a natural progression. At first she'd picked up litter from the grounds or swept the floor of the center on weekends. Slowly, she'd gained the trust of the nature center's state-employed manager, and eventually Chelsea found herself caring for the wounded animals that were invariably brought to the center wrapped in towels or dropped off outside the door in shoe boxes.

Most of the animals cared for at the shelter were unfortunate victims of fast-moving traffic. Then there were animals, like the squirrel, who had gotten themselves into some other kind of trouble. The actual medical care of the wild animals was seen to by a veterinarian who donated his time on an "as needed" basis.

The hours she spent volunteering at the center were a joy for Chelsea. The animals she tended helped fill the emotional void inside her. The helpless creatures she fed and watered gave her an outlet for the love, kindness and caring she guarded so fiercely when it came to humans.

It was safe for her to pour all the compassion she felt into taking care of the birds, chipmunks, raccoons, squirrels and other forest creatures that found themselves in need of help. It was safe because Chelsea knew from the beginning of each animal's internment that there would come a time when the creature would be set free. She knew up front that each relationship was short-term—that one day the animal would scamper off into the underbrush, never to be seen again.

Never to be seen again. The words brought an image to her mind. A sharp, painful image from the past.

"Mama Higgins," she whispered, her voice throaty with poignant emotion. Sudden tears burned behind her lids, but she dashed the back of her hand across her eyes, refusing to allow them to fall. Chelsea shoved the thought from her mind, inhaled deeply and cleared her throat.

But what had pulled that distant memory to the surface of her brain? She strongly suspected it was because she'd made herself vulnerable to Ben. Disclosing to him her desire to have a baby had forced a crack in the wall she'd painstakingly built around her emotions—a crack that had obviously widened enough to let out the painful memory of the woman from her past.

Don't let the memories escape, she commanded silently. Just push them down deep, and keep them there.

A beautiful blue jay perched in the next cage, its tail feathers slightly tattered. As Chelsea worked to install a small seed-covered suet ball in the cage, the bird never stirred, so exhausted by its earlier ordeal.

Chelsea stroked the bird's tiny head. From the note near the cage, she learned that the jay had flown into the picture window of a house near the nature center.

"Poor fella," she crooned. "How were you to know the window was covered with a pane of glass?"

The birds were the hardest for her to part with. The center kept numerous bird feeders filled all through the year. She often wondered if any of the winged creatures that came to feed were the ones she'd previously cared for and had come to love. But she never dwelled on the thought, because she always reminded herself that she had known from the first that the animals she tended didn't belong to her. They would be returned to the wild as soon as they had healed.

That was the same way she must view this temporary relationship with Ben. Once they spoke the vows of marriage, she'd be his wife—for a while.

It was going to be imperative for her to be on her guard at all times. She couldn't afford to become involved with Ben on any kind of emotional level. She knew so well what would happen if she did. Heartwrenching pain. Humiliation. Unbearable sorrow. It had happened so often in her younger years. She wouldn't let it happen again. She couldn't. For if it did, she knew she wouldn't survive.

Without thinking, Chelsea rubbed the flat of her palm across her taut lower abdomen. She would become Ben's wife, and she would sleep with him—no matter how difficult it would be. Because doing so would bring her a baby.

A baby on whom she could pour every ounce of love she felt. A baby who would love her unconditionally. A baby unable to inflict hurt. A baby she could care for and love and never, ever, *ever* abandon—

Chelsea gasped and abolished the thought—a thought that came too close to completely demolishing the wall that held back her horrible memories. She shook her head.

Her emotions were in such turmoil. First, Mama Higgins had come to mind, and now she'd remembered that other woman, the hated, despicable one who had caused her such pain. It had been many long months since those memories had plagued her.

It had to be this situation with Ben that was causing these awful recollections. Her offer to marry him—for a price—had shaken her more than she'd first imagined.

Their drive into Elkton in order to register for a marriage license had been a trip fraught with awkwardness and emotions that she'd had to take great pains to hide.

Oh, it had all seemed superficial enough. The two of them had shared mundane conversation about the beautiful limestone carving on the facade of the old courthouse, several ducks taking flight above marsh reeds, a fat trout jumping out of the water. Ben had explained to her how the carving was supposed to have been an exact replica of the county seal, but the artist had added the fish without consulting the town's officials.

The two of them had chuckled together self-consciously about how nervous the other registering couples looked. Ben had commented how the two of them needn't feel the least bit nervous.

But despite Ben's attempts to trivialize the act, registering for their marriage license only seemed to emphasize the fact that he *was* nervous—terribly nervous. And although she hadn't meant to, she'd found herself empathizing with him.

Then doubt had planted itself between his brows in a deep frown and Chelsea had begun to wonder things—what he was thinking, was he reconsidering the terms of their deal, was he going to back out at the last minute, how handsome he is—

The last thought had stunned her. Why the heck had she noticed his looks? It had nothing to do with their bargain.

Yes, she'd discovered that Ben evoked responses in her that were surprising. But that was okay, as long as she could hide those responses. As long as she showed him no emotion. As long as she didn't come to care. That would only result in her becoming vulnerable, and vulnerability was her dreaded enemy.

If she simply controlled herself, if she kept her cool reserve, she'd be fine. She could do this.

Ben maneuvered his truck slowly along the narrow, curving country road. Every morning he picked up his aunt and drove her to Reed's Orchard Country Store where she sold the fruits that he grew. Every evening he drove her home.

"Why are you so quiet tonight?" May asked.

"No reason," he answered automatically. Then, he couldn't help chuckling. "Do you realize what's happened to me today?"

"Sure do," May said. "We're getting married."

"*I'm* getting married." He ran his fingers through his hair as he'd already done dozens of times today in his quest to figure out this situation he found himself in. "I can hardly believe it."

"I can hardly believe Chelsea offered." May cut her eyes at her nephew. "But, then again, she won't be walking away empty-handed."

"No," Ben said. "She won't."

"Oooowhee. You've not only saved the orchard, but you'll be making love to a beautiful woman."

"May." Ben's tone held a warning.

"You can't tell me you don't think she's beautiful," May said. "Why those big brown doe eyes would melt any man's heart."

"I'm not in this to have my heart melted."

Ben turned onto the gravel driveway that flanked May's one-story brick ranch house.

"I know," May said, patting Ben on the arm. "But don't fret so. Everything will work out just fine." She got out of the truck and slammed the door. Leaning in through the passenger-side window, she grinningly added, "And, who knows? You might even enjoy yourself."

She laughed mischievously and started off toward her front door.

Ben watched, shaking his head at her remark, until his aunt was inside. As he drove toward home, he tried to focus on May's assurance that everything would work out fine.

He hoped she was right about that. But her other prediction was dead wrong. Ben was certain he wouldn't enjoy himself.

Chapter Three

"We are gathered here—"

Chelsea watched the clerk's lips as they formed the words of the wedding ceremony, but no sound seemed to emanate from them. All she could hear was the fierce pounding of her heart and the whoosh of blood rushing through her ears.

"To join this man and this woman—"

Radiant morning sunbeams streamed through the office window, auguring a bright future for this marriage—but how could that be, Chelsea wondered, when this union was not based on love? A deep, all-encompassing melancholy enveloped her, despite the fact that she knew she *should* be feeling happy, relieved even, to finally be achieving her dream.

"The contract of marriage is a most solemn one—"

Casting a side glance at Ben, she marveled at how his bloodred tie stood out so vividly against the pristine whiteness of his shirt. His handsome face seemed devoid of emotion.

"Not to be entered into lightly—"

Chelsea turned her head and locked her gaze onto the plain wooden lectern separating Ben and her from the circuit-court clerk. She knew the apprehension and confusion churning through her was caused by a mixture of fatigue and second thoughts. Sleep had eluded her last night as she'd been bombarded by doubts.

"But thoughtfully and seriously—"

Had she been crazy to offer this deal to Ben, she wondered. She was going to live with the man. Why, she was going to be *intimate* with him. Before last night, she'd refused to think about the physical aspects involved between a man and woman that were necessary to procreate—the physical aspects, which she and Ben would perform.

"With a deep realization of its obligations—"

The dark wood paneling absorbed the strong morning sunlight and warmed the air to a stifling degree. She felt claustrophobic and had to fight the urge to tug at the collar of her new cream-colored dress. She craved some fresh air and longed to be back in the wide-open spaces of the orchard.

"Anyone can show just cause why they should not be lawfully joined—"

The request seeped into her subconscious. *Because we don't love each other,* came her silent response. But then, Chelsea had known going into this marriage that Ben would never—could never—love her the way a husband should love a wife. But that wasn't his fault. However, the words tumbled through her head: How was she going to bring herself to sleep with a man who didn't love her?

"Let him speak now or forever hold his peace."

Before continuing with the ceremony, the clerk shot Chelsea a reassuring smile and Chelsea tried hard to return it, but her facial muscles, seemingly numb, refused to obey her command.

"Ben Danvers, will you take Chelsea Carson for your lawful wife?"

"I will."

Chelsea came alive at the sound of Ben's rich, steady voice. Her breath caught in her throat and she couldn't bring herself to look at him.

"Chelsea Carson, will you take Ben Danvers for your lawful husband?"

Her spine was so stiff, she felt as though it might shatter into a million pieces. *You will do this,* she silently commanded. If you want to conceive a child, then you *will* marry Ben. You *will* sleep with him.

"Your response should be, 'I will,'" the clerk gently coached her.

She forced herself to look at Ben. "I will," she said, and marveled at how even her voice sounded.

Ben's jaw clenched as he observed Chelsea's cool, composed demeanor. Nerves were jumping in his gut like a jackhammer. Did she feel no emotion? Was she so coldhearted that she could pledge herself without batting an eye to a man for whom she felt nothing? How was it that this woman he was taking as his wife could be so dispassionate?

"Please join hands."

Ben felt the silken pads of Chelsea's fingertips slide across his calloused palm.

"To have and to hold," he repeated after the clerk, his voice rough with the anxiety churning inside him, "from this day forward, for better, for worse, for richer, for poorer, in sickness and in health, until death do us part."

He looked into Chelsea's eyes and remembered his aunt's description of "big, brown doe eyes" that would "melt any man's heart." He wondered if there was anything that could melt Chelsea's.

"To have and to hold—"

As he stood there, quietly listening to her repeat the vow, Ben became aware of the subtle trembling of her fingers and a sense of confusion settled in his brow.

"From this day forward, for better, for worse, for richer, for poorer, in sickness and in health . . . until death do us part."

She actually whispered the last phrase and there was something in her tone that he couldn't quite read. Ben's frown deepened, but he hadn't time to think about the revelation fluttering at the edges of his brain before the clerk was signaling him to slide the thin gold band on the third finger of Chelsea's left hand.

"With this ring, I thee wed," he said.

Chelsea slipped a matching gold band over his work-roughened knuckle. "With this ring, I thee wed." She repeated the words without raising her gaze from the shiny ring on his hand.

The two of them turned to face the clerk and were once again instructed to join hands.

"I now pronounce you husband and wife."

Looking down at his wife's face, Ben felt nearly crushed with a sudden need to thank her—to somehow show this woman just how indebted he felt that she would give him so much.

"Thanks, Chelsea," he murmured. And feeling that words were inadequate, he slowly leaned forward and pressed his lips against hers.

Chelsea was utterly and completely astonished by the heat curling in her stomach when she felt Ben's warm, gentle kiss. A stentorian warning bell of self-preservation jarred her into jerking away from him and the wonderful feeling he evoked in her.

Averting her gaze, she replied, "You're welcome."

Her curt, icy tone was like a douse of cold water on the tender emotions he'd been feeling. He could have sworn just a moment earlier Chelsea had actually been feeling... had been feeling... What? he asked himself.

Curling his index finger under her chin, he lifted her face so he could look into her eyes. The cool brown orbs stared at him with no trace of softness—all he saw was unemotional composure.

"Come on," he told her gruffly. "Let's get out of here."

They went up the stairs and out into the parking lot in complete silence. Ben opened the passenger-side door for her and she got into his pickup. She watched him circle the truck and slide into the cab.

He sighed heavily as he jabbed the key into the ignition. But before he started the engine, he turned to her.

"I really do want to thank you," he said.

He means it, she thought. He really means it. She started to smile at him, but stopped herself. There was danger in the emotions Ben conjured in her. She couldn't allow herself to care for him—couldn't allow herself to become vulnerable to him in any way.

"And I'll really thank you," she forced herself to say, "when you fulfill your end of the deal."

Ben only nodded curtly before he started the truck and headed home.

Chelsea placed her hairbrush and comb on the dresser of the small bedroom that, for a while at least, she'd call her own. After the civil ceremony this morning, Chelsea had assured Ben she didn't need help moving her few things into his home. Although he seemed reluctant, she finally persuaded him to go ahead with his work, and she told him they could meet at his house that evening for dinner.

So she had spent the previous hour or so hanging blouses and skirts in the closet, folding jeans, socks and underclothes and tucking them away in drawers.

Glancing first at her wristwatch and then out the window at the dusky sky, she decided Ben would be coming home soon and it was time to start supper. She wasn't much of a cook—she'd only had time to learn one or two recipes from Mama Higgins before—

Immediately, she squashed the memory. This wasn't a time for sadness. Jubilation was the order of the day, and she would feel joy if it killed her.

But the giddy nerves in the pit of her stomach refused to stop their frenzied dancing. And the anxious questions wouldn't quit pestering her mind. How was she going to approach Ben about fulfilling his end of the deal? Would she even have to? Or would he "perform" without any prompting from her?

A hysterical giggle nearly escaped her at the thought of that last question.

Then she frowned. What if he didn't want to do "it" tonight? Or tomorrow night? What if...?

"Now, you're being downright silly," she said to her reflection in the mirror. Of course he'd want to do it.

From everything she'd ever read about men, they loved to do it. They lived to do it. Why, the television talk shows depicted men as extremely lustful creatures. She was certain she wouldn't have any problem with Ben when it came to having sex.

But did she really have enough nerve to... to actually...? She couldn't even bring herself to think about what it was she and Ben were going to do. But she'd find the will to do it, nonetheless. She would.

Leaning closer to the glass, Chelsea whispered, "A twenty-eight-year-old virgin. He'll never believe it."

Well, he'd simply have to believe it, she thought, pushing herself away from the dresser and walking down the hallway and into the kitchen. He'd have proof in the end, when they finally... did it. Chelsea brushed her hand across her forehead at the thought. This wasn't something she was looking forward to. But it was necessary.

Opening the refrigerator, she pulled out an onion, the grated cheese and the sweet Italian sausage she'd bought earlier, and put her energies into making a casserole.

Thirty minutes later the pasta and meat were cooked, and the casserole was in the oven. Chelsea had turned her attention to setting the table when she heard the front door open.

"Hi, honey, I'm home!" Ben called.

Chelsea's hand froze, the dinner knife a scant inch from its proper place beside the plate.

He was still chuckling when he walked into the kitchen. Taking one look at her unsmiling face, his shoulders sagged. "It was a joke, Chelsea. Just a joke."

She nodded, but couldn't bring herself to smile. Of course it was a joke. No one would ever call her a pet name such as "honey" and mean it.

"Dinner will be ready soon," she said.

"I don't expect you to cook my meals."

"Well—" she shrugged "—I have to eat, too, you know. The dish I made may not be much, but you're welcome to share it."

"I wasn't implying that I didn't want to share the food...." He let the sentence trail and stared at her. Then he sighed. "I'll just go take a quick shower." He disappeared down the hall.

When they sat at the table to eat, an awkward silence settled down with them. Chelsea lifted the lid off the casserole dish and the fragrant aroma of sausage and tomato sauce wafted through the kitchen.

Ben inhaled deeply. "I'm starved," he said.

Without replying, she spooned him a large helping of the baked pasta and sliced a piece of warm, crusty bread.

"Did you bake this?" he asked, indicating the loaf of bread.

"No, I just heated it through."

She served herself and sat down to eat. But her curiosity made it hard to keep her eyes on her plate. She wanted to look at him—wanted to watch his mannerisms as he ate. Was he enjoying the food she'd prepared? Did he—?

"So, how was your day?"

Chelsea jumped at his question. "Fine," she answered.

After a moment, Ben asked, "So, what did you do this afternoon?"

She shrugged one shoulder. "Nothing."

He looked at her for several long seconds—seconds during which her nerves had ample time to become frayed as she wondered what he was thinking.

Finally, he set down his fork and rested his elbows on the table.

She could stand his scrutiny no longer. "What?" she asked.

"I'm trying to make some friendly conversation here."

"Oh." Chelsea swallowed a bite of bread. "My day was fine." Picking up her fork, she speared a slice of spicy sausage and lifted it toward her mouth.

"Well?" he asked.

Her hand froze, the fork hovering directly in front of her face.

"Aren't you going to ask me about my day?"

She hadn't thought to return the question.

"Chelsea, people who live together and spend time together talk to one another." He wiped the corner of his mouth with a napkin. "Okay, so it may be pointless and useless conversation, but it's conversation nevertheless."

Taking the meat between her teeth, she chewed thoughtfully. After a moment she gazed at him. "So," she said after she swallowed, "how was your day?"

Ben grinned. "That wasn't so hard, was it?" He reached for a second slice of bread and slathered it with butter. "My day was good. I got a lot done. There are enough trees on the orchard to keep me busy pruning eleven months out of the year, and that's no exaggeration. But you know that already, don't you?"

Chelsea nodded in response.

"I finished up the Barn Grove today. I'll have the crew move on to Old Lew's Place tomorrow." He stopped a moment to take a drink of iced tea. "I'll go out there with the men for a while, then I'll come back to the office to catch up on some paperwork."

Again, she nodded, but silence quickly fell between them again.

Ben slid his elbow off the table's edge and picked up his fork. "You can jump right in on this conversation any time you like."

Keeping to herself most of the time, Chelsea wasn't well practiced in the art of friendly conversation. She did see a few other volunteers at the nature center now and then, but talk there usually centered around the animals or work that needed doing. She went to church every Sunday, but there she said nothing more than "hello" and "goodbye" and "see you next week." She cleared her throat.

"Is it hard?" she asked, her voice tentative.

"What? The pruning?" Ben shook his head. "Naw. Since Granddad and I planted all the dwarf trees, pruning is fairly easy. Just takes a few quick snips." One corner of his mouth curled. "It's just that there's so many darn trees to snip."

Chelsea nodded and suddenly felt pressured for something else to ask.

"Um...how did the different groves get to be named?" She swallowed nervously, wondering if it was a dumb question. She rushed to explain, so he wouldn't think her completely stupid. "I mean, I know the Barn Grove is named for the big red barn out in the middle of the orchard. But what about the grove you call Old Lew's Place? Or Devon's Place? Or...or Accident Acre?"

He leaned back in his chair. "Most of the groves are named after the people we bought the land from," he said. "Granddad bought Old Lew's Place from Old Lew years and years ago. Old Lew was nearly a hundred years old at the time and didn't want to sell, but he became too ill to farm, so he sold his land to Granddad. Granddad bought Devon's Place from Richard Devon while I was still in college." Then he chuckled. "Now, Accident Acre is another story. Granddad bought that small parcel of ground before I was born. Three men were hurt as they were clearing off the scrub brush. So Granddad referred to it as Accident Acre."

"Oh," she said.

The panic that crawled in her stomach as she searched for something—anything—to say must have showed on her face because Ben slid out his chair, stood and picked up his plate. On his way to the sink, he asked, "You're really not used to this, are you?"

"Not used to what?" she asked, even though she knew very well what he was referring to.

"Talking." He turned to face her.

She dipped her head low, not wanting him to witness her embarrassment. She saw her hands in her lap, her fingers clenching the napkin tightly. "No, I'm not," she quietly admitted. "But I'll try harder."

The invisible touch of his green eyes made her lift her gaze to his. She saw him smile gently.

"It's okay," he said. "We'll get used to each other."

He came over to stand beside her and covered her hand with his. And even though Chelsea knew this was a gesture of reassurance on his part, she automatically distanced herself from him, slipping her fingers from underneath his. She didn't want to push him away, but a habit learned from years of emotional survival was impossible to deny.

Awkwardness surrounded them like a thick fog. Chelsea tried to ignore it by busying herself with the task of clearing the table.

"I'll do this," Ben told her, taking the salt-and-pepper shakers from her hands. "You cooked. It's only fair that I clean up. Go on into the other room and relax. Prop your feet up."

Chelsea was relieved for an excuse to leave the room. She sat down on the sofa, picked up a magazine and absently thumbed through the pages, not seeing the informative articles or the colorful advertisements.

Why did Ben have to be so...nice? He was a good person, a wonderful man. And she'd found it hard not to look at him. She wanted badly to deny that she found him handsome—that she was attracted to his sun-bleached hair, his jewel green eyes, his easy smile.

She heard the water running as he rinsed off the plates and utensils; the glasses clinked together as he loaded them into the dishwasher.

Thoughts of what the two of them would do later this evening forced their way into her mind. It was hard for her to imagine going to bed with such a beautiful man. She had no experience, other than the television shows and movies she'd seen and books she'd read. But she and Ben wouldn't be engaging in the soft, passionate lovemaking depicted in romance movies and novels. No, Chelsea expected hers to be a quick, unemotional coupling.

Just then Ben came into the room with an uncorked bottle of wine and two stemmed glasses.

"I thought a little of this magic elixir would help us to relax," he said.

He poured the rich red wine into one glass and handed it to her. As he poured one for himself, he commented, "I should have thought to serve it with that delicious dinner."

"Oh, that's okay," she said. But a tiny burst of joy exploded inside her at his compliment.

When he sat down next to her, Chelsea instinctively inched away from him toward the arm of the sofa.

"Boy, am I tired," he said. "I've had a long day."

Disappointment welled inside her, hot and strong. "Too tired?"

Ben looked at her, a puzzled frown crossing his features. He realized her implication at the same moment she realized she'd actually asked. Her hand flew up to cover her mouth, her eyes wide with embarrassment.

He laughed softly and shook his head. "It's okay. I understand. And, no, I'm not that tired."

The two of them sat there and Chelsea could feel the silence that she'd embraced all her adult life swiftly becoming her enemy.

"So, what do we drink to?"

His question took her off guard. "Drink to?" she asked.

"Chelsea, we're in the middle of a successful campaign here," he said. "We've accomplished one of our goals by saving Reed's Orchard from being sold." His green eyes darkened and his mouth tipped into an off-center smile. "Don't you think we should drink to the *complete* success of our deal?"

She knew he was speaking of her successful pregnancy. Forcing a smile, she said, "Well . . . sure."

"To success," he said, and lightly tapped the rim of his glass to hers. She watched him take a deep swallow and then she took a tiny sip. The wine tasted fruity and slightly sweet and it trailed a warm path down her throat.

He reached behind her and turned down the brightness of the lamp on the end table. Chelsea's spine straightened so quickly she sloshed wine onto the back of her hand.

"Ohhh, look what I've done," she said. What the heck was he doing?

"Atmosphere."

His answer told her she'd spoken the question aloud.

"But ... but ..."

"It's okay," he assured her gently. "We don't have to do anything right away. Let's just get comfortable. Let's just relax."

He took the wineglass from her hand and set it on the coffee table. She hadn't noticed when he'd set his down, but he had. He took her fingers in his and pulled them toward him.

"But I've spilled the wine," she protested, panic rising in her chest, and she weakly tried to pull her hand to her.

"Oh, but I have the perfect remedy for that," he murmured, his voice tinged with wickedness.

Slowly, his lips touched the back of her hand and he gently sucked the wine from her skin.

For the second time that day Chelsea felt a slowing down of time. No, this was a complete cessation of life as she knew it. Ben's tongue was like warm velvet against her flesh. His lips sent a delicious heat radiating up her arm.

Because his head was bent, she wasn't able to see exactly what he was doing. It felt as though he kissed the tender spot between her index finger and thumb. The tip of his nose brushed back and forth across her tingling skin. He sniffed gently and deeply, and the muscles in her stomach tightened almost painfully.

Why...why he was inhaling her scent! She found that fact extremely erotic. Although she felt sluggish and giddily drunk, she knew it had nothing to do with the wine. She was actually feeling...sensual.

The realization made her gasp and she snatched her hand from his grasp.

"What are you doing?" The words sounded as strangled as she felt.

He lifted his head to gaze at her, his green eyes holding a mixture of perplexity and some other dark, mysterious emotion she was afraid to identify.

"Well," he began. "I guess I'm trying to...turn you on...get you in the mood...arouse you."

She blinked several times. "Is that absolutely necessary?"

Ben leaned back against the couch and rubbed his jaw in contemplation. He darted a look at her, then another. Finally, he said, "No, I guess it's not. But, then, I guess we should talk about this."

"Do we have to?" This time her question sounded squeaky to her ears and Chelsea was so mortified she wanted to hide her face in her hands. But she forced herself to finish. "Can't we just...you know...do it?"

She watched his frown deepen.

"Seeing as the two of us have differing ideas as to how we should 'do it,'" he said, "I don't see how we can get around talking about it."

Chelsea's lips set in a grim line.

He sighed heavily and glanced toward the ceiling. When his gaze returned to her face he said, "Okay. Let's take this slow. There's no reason to be embarrassed, we're both adults. We know what has to happen in order for you to get pregnant." He hesitated a moment. Then his tone became quite soft as he asked, "How *did* you want us—" he indicated the two of them with a back-and-forth movement of his hand "—to go about making love?"

Closing her eyes at the sound of his last two words, she did her best to calm her pounding heartbeat. She slowly raised her eyelids and took a deep breath.

"What we'll be doing certainly can't be called . . . making love," she said stiffly.

"Oh? And what is it called?"

Chelsea swallowed nervously. "We'll be . . . well, we'll be . . . procreating." Her face flared hot as the word passed her lips and she was forced to look away from him.

His eyebrows raised high. "Sounds kind of clinical," he remarked.

When she made no response, he asked, "How does this procreation work?"

Her gaze flew to his face. "Ben." The tone of her voice and her agonized expression implored him not to force her to explain.

"Oh, I understand the intimate nuances of the act itself," he said, ignoring her silent plea. "But I would like you to clarify the preliminary details involved in your plan."

"Preliminary details?" Chelsea searched his face for some sign to tell her he really wasn't going to insist on a description, but he only settled back against the sofa to await her answer.

Clearing her throat, she took a shaky breath. "Okay, well," she began slowly, "I thought we'd go

back there—'' she pointed down the hallway to indi-
cate the bedroom ''—and take off...'' Here her voice
failed her and she simply fingered the collar of her
blouse to convey her message. She ran her tongue over
her dry lips. "And then...I thought we'd get into
the..." Her voice turned quavery and she closed her
eyes as she hurriedly stated her last thoughts. "Then
we'd have...well, we'd have..."

Realizing she simply couldn't bring herself to finish
the sentence, she clamped her mouth shut and turned
her head away.

"Chelsea." His voice was gentle. "Look at me."

When she did, she saw that his expression was just
as gentle as his tone.

"Chelsea, this is what you're trying to say. You
want us to go back to the *bedroom*. You want us to
take off our *clothes*. You want us to get into the *bed*.
And you want us to have *intercourse*." He took her
hand in his. "Tell me how you expect to do those
things, when you can't even bring yourself to say the
words."

"I want to have a baby," she whispered. "I'll do
whatever I have to."

"But do you want the memory of conceiving your
child to be so cold...so clinical as what you seem to
have in mind?"

"Ben, two people do not have to be in love to make
a baby." Chelsea pushed back the wall of emotion that
threatened to pen her in.

"No, we don't have to be in love," he agreed. "But
is there some reason we can't at least enjoy our-
selves?"

Before she could answer, he continued, "Chelsea this can be a warm and happy experience for us both."

"I don't need to enjoy myself. It's not necessary for me to have an—" She stopped suddenly and shifted her gaze to the floor. "I don't have to enjoy myself to conceive a child."

"*Orgasm*, Chelsea," he said. "The word you're looking for is orgasm. And you're right, it isn't necessary for you to have an orgasm to conceive."

Chelsea pulled her hand from his and slid back even farther into the corner of the sofa.

"But," he said, his tone a bit harder, "it *is* necessary for *me* to have an orgasm if you're to become pregnant. I'm not a stud horse. I'm not an animal. I'm a human being—a man with feelings and emotions."

Feeling as though she would choke on the panic that churned in her chest, Chelsea placed the flat of her palm at the base of her throat.

"Look at me, Chels."

She slowly raised her eyes to his and felt unshed tears burning the backs of her eyelids. She would not lose control. She would not!

"It really isn't fair of you," he said, "to expect me to reveal the most intimate part of myself to you when you aren't willing to reveal the most intimate part of yourself to me."

"Oh, so it's 'you show me yours and I'll show you mine,' huh?" She knew very well she was being unfair to him—knew her question was mean spirited—but her words were an ingrained self-defense mechanism that she was unable to stop.

"This has nothing to do with physical body parts and you know it," he said. "This has to do with feelings—the most intimate of feelings."

"Feelings." Chelsea spat the word out in a way that was certain to convey her disgust. She wanted to make him angry. She wanted to make him shout at her, make him call her names, anything rather than talk about this subject any longer. She was afraid that if they continued down this avenue she would surely fall apart.

"I'm not going to fight about this," he said calmly. "It's obvious that you don't trust me. And until you do—" he slid his hand down his thigh and cupped it over his knee "—I don't see how it would be possible for us sleep together."

"But that's not fair!" Chelsea sat up straight, her gaze locking with his. "We made a deal. You said you'd make me pregnant."

"And I'm not saying I won't," he said. "I have no intention of backing out of our deal. But I'm going to have to add a stipulation of my own."

"You're going to force me to...enjoy myself?" she asked, her tone tight with suppressed emotion.

He obviously couldn't help the smile that gently curled his mouth. "No," he said, shaking his head. "All I'm asking is that we get to know one another. I want you to know who's making love to you. And I want to know who I'm making love to." Then his gaze intensified, as he added, "I want you to trust me."

"But... but..."

He touched her thigh with his strong, tanned hand. "It won't take long, Chels. You'll see. Soon you'll understand that I'm not a bad person. I only want to help you the way you've helped me." He stood up and looked down at her. "Good night, Chels. I'll see you in the morning."

She silently watched him cross the room, heard his footsteps fade down the hallway. Every muscle in her body felt stretched to the limit. Tears screamed for release.

He didn't know what he was asking. She knew he wasn't a bad person. In fact, she'd already noticed just how wonderful he was. But she couldn't get to know him. She couldn't let him get to know her. And she certainly couldn't ever come to trust him. Because that would mean she'd have to reveal herself to him. And Chelsea knew revealing herself meant becoming vulnerable.

Her chin quivered and a single tear trailed slowly down her cheek. Vulnerable was the one thing she'd long ago promised herself she'd never become.

Chapter Four

Ben sat at the kitchen table lingering over his morning coffee. It had been three days since his wedding—three days since he and Chelsea had discussed their differing views on sleeping together. And now he felt as though they were at some sort of stalemate. She'd been standoffish toward him before this whole marriage business, but now she avoided him altogether. That's why he'd decided to dawdle a bit this morning and have an unprecedented second cup of coffee, in an effort to force her to talk to him.

He felt bad about insisting on their getting to know one another before they tried to conceive a baby. He knew that physiologically it wasn't necessary for them to know or even like one another before they made love. But Chelsea had made the act sound so impersonal, so clinical. He couldn't imagine having sex with an unresponsive woman.

Ben found that idea humiliating, although he felt Chelsea didn't intend him to feel that way. He realized that her intense desire to become pregnant was blinding her to the fact that they were two human beings—human beings with emotions that needed to be recognized and dealt with. The scenario she painted seemed wrong to him. It felt wrong, and he refused to be a part of it.

He really couldn't understand Chelsea. She obviously wanted a baby very much, but she didn't seem to show the loving and caring emotions he thought would be necessary to parent a child.

Doubting Chelsea's abilities as a mother brought to mind a question that he hadn't thought of before: How did he feel about becoming a father? The circumstances under which he would be fathering this child were so strange that he really couldn't explain how he felt. Chelsea had made it very clear that she didn't want his active participation as a parent. He'd have to learn to live with the fact that he would be a father, but he wouldn't be a *father*. He frowned at the emptiness that the thought left him with.

More than anything, he had to realize that neither Chelsea's mothering instincts nor his thoughts of being a daddy should be his concern. He'd struck a deal with Chelsea, and he knew he must fulfill his end. And he planned to, just as soon as he and Chelsea could feel comfortable enough with each other to engage in the intimacies of sex.

The phone rang and he picked up the receiver.

"Hello?"

"Ben, it's May. Is Chelsea there?"

"Yes—"

"Is she awake?" May asked, her tone a bit frantic.

"She's up," he said. "I heard her rummaging around in her room. What's wrong, Aunt May?"

"I really need to talk to her."

"Okay," he said. "I'll call her to the phone."

Ben set down the phone receiver and went to fetch Chelsea. On his way through the house, he wondered why May would be calling Chelsea. As far as he knew the two of them were little more than working acquaintances—but then, now that he thought about it, Chelsea didn't seem to have any close friends. Everyone seemed to be an acquaintance to her. She didn't seem to let anyone into that invisible circle that was so tightly drawn around her.

He stopped outside Chelsea's bedroom and knocked.

She opened the wooden door, but Ben could clearly see from the expression on her face that the invisible door of tension that had been between them since their wedding night was locked tight into place.

"I thought you had left for work," she said.

Ben shook his head. "May's on the phone."

"For me?" Her brow furrowed.

"Um-hmm."

He stood there in the hallway and watched her walk away from him. His eyes were drawn down the length of her retreating figure. Her shiny chestnut hair hung loose, the soft curls at the ends bouncing with each step. The supple fabric of her well-worn jeans hugged her hips and thighs like butter on bread. And those hips swayed gently from side to side. He could tell her modest sashay was not intentional, but was induced by a visceral femininity. One corner of his mouth pulled into a tiny grin as he realized just how appealing he found the natural provocative movement of her body.

She rounded the corner and disappeared from his view, but his imagination easily took over and he envisioned himself intimately embracing his wife. He crossed his arms, leaned against the doorjamb and let the image take shape. Her big brown eyes gazed up at him lovingly, and he ran his fingers along her jaw and down the silky alabaster skin of her neck. He wondered if she might gasp and throw back her head if he slid his palm even lower, over the full roundness of her breast. He imagined her eyes fluttering closed as he kissed her mouth. Closing his own eyes, he felt his heartbeat quicken as he fantasized about how her naked body would feel pressed against his, her hands playing over him, kneading his chest, his stomach, in a slow, erotic motion that stirred him—

"Ben?"

He snapped to attention. "What?" Startled from his reverie by the sound of Chelsea's voice, he knew his answer was a couple decibels louder than necessary. He was relieved that the shadowy hallway would hide the blaze of embarrassment that must surely be written all over his face.

A curious look crept across Chelsea's features, but thankfully she didn't ask him what he was doing standing there with a stupid, lustful smirk on his face.

For once, Ben was a tad grateful for his wife's cool, aloof nature.

"I have to go over to May's," Chelsea told him.

"Is something wrong?"

"There's a bird or something trapped in her chimney."

She swiped a lock of hair back from her face, and a deep disappointment shot through him knowing that the tenebrous shadows that hid his embarrassment a moment ago would keep him from seeing her dark eyes up close right now.

"It's probably a squirrel," he said.

"She said she thought she heard wings flapping."

"Oh." He frowned. "Could be a bat."

She nodded. "May called an exterminator who said he could come right out but that he couldn't guarantee the creature's safety. So she called me, knowing I spend a lot of time around animals at the nature center."

The lock of dark hair fell onto her cheek again and Ben had to force himself not to reach up and tuck it behind her ear.

"I called the center," she continued. "But there's no one there this early. I'll go to May's myself and see what I can do. But I told her I couldn't promise that the animal wouldn't be hurt by my efforts to get him out of the chimney, either."

Her mouth curled into a tiny, rare smile and Ben found it alluring, so alluring in fact that he wanted to say something that would make that special smile widen even farther.

"The thing is," he said gently, "that you'll have its welfare in mind more than any exterminator would."

One corner of her lips did draw back a little more, but only for an instant before she nodded and turned away.

"Wait," he said. "I'll go with you."

"Oh, that's not necessary."

"But I want to," he told her. "And if you don't mind, I'd like for us to spend a little time together today."

"But your work..." she protested.

He shrugged one shoulder. "It's Saturday. I deserve some time off. I really would like to spend some time with you." Then a little hesitantly he added, "If you don't mind."

She dipped her head so he couldn't see her face and he fought the urge to reach out and tilt up her chin with his fingertips.

"I don't mind," she said.

Ben's spirit soared and he felt he'd somehow won a small battle.

Half an hour later, Ben watched his wife kneel close to May's fireplace and look up into the chimney.

"I don't see anything." Her voice was muffled.

"Maybe it flew out already," May said. "I haven't heard anything for a while."

Chelsea thumped on the inside wall of the chimney. "There he is!" she called. She ducked out of the fireplace. "I can see him now, but he's too far up for me to reach. He's perched on the edge of a rough brick or something up there and he's not moving much. I hope he's not hurt."

Her face was so intent. She swiped at her bangs and smudged her temple with the creosote that stained her fingers. *She's a beautiful woman,* Ben thought. The observation entered his head in such a natural manner that it surprised him.

"I'll go up on the roof—"

"No," he cut her off. "I'll go up."

"Maybe if we leave the bird alone it will just fly out," May said.

Chelsea shook her head. "He can't. Birds fly on air currents. They can't maneuver like a helicopter, flying straight up. No, he's stuck all right."

"I'll see if I can reach it from the roof," Ben offered.

"You'd better take a broom or something with a long handle," Chelsea said. "If you can't reach him, you'll have to nudge him off his perch and I'll try to catch him down here in the hearth."

"I'm glad I called you," May commented. "It sounds like you've done this before."

"Actually, I haven't," she said. "But I'll be careful."

Ben positioned the ladder against the side of the house and climbed the rungs with May's best straw broom in one hand, a flashlight tucked in his pocket. He carefully crawled onto the gritty asphalt roof tiles, stood up and made his way to where the chimney rose above the house.

Peering down into the dark recesses of the flue, Ben decided he needed the flashlight. He directed the beam and quickly found a small owl perched inside the chimney.

"I see it," he called down to Chelsea.

"Can you reach him?"

He reached his arm inside as far as he could. He felt along the sides of the flue and pulled his hand free.

"Yuck." Wrinkling his nose, he called down, "Chels, tell May it's time to have her chimney cleaned."

The sound of Chelsea's light laughter filtered up toward him and he stopped short. Granted, it hadn't been much of a laugh, hardly a chuckle really, but he realized that this had been the first time he'd ever heard it. He found the sound of it delightful and wanted badly to hear it again.

"I'm a mess." He directed his statement so she could hear.

He was rewarded with another tinkling of her laughter and she said, "Welcome to the club."

His chest filled with a warmth he would have thought impossible when it came to Chelsea. And he found it a marvelous revelation.

"I'm going to use the broom handle," Ben said.

"Gently, Ben," she called softly. "Please remember that he's scared."

Ever so slowly, he lowered the broom, handle side down, into the flue. It took only a tiny nudge. The owl gave a frightened shriek and plummeted into the blackness.

There was a commotion of flapping wings and screeches from the bird, and Ben's heart hammered in his chest when he heard Chelsea scream.

"Chelsea?"

She didn't answer.

When she screamed a second time, he jerked the broom from the chimney and it landed on the roof with a thump.

"Chelsea!" he yelled.

Ben scrambled toward the ladder and climbed down as fast as he safely could. He rounded the house and burst through the front door.

The sight before him shocked him into speechlessness. Chelsea was gently cradling the small owl in her hands. She crooned soothingly, and the comfort in her tone, the expression of concern on her face was all-consuming. It was clearly evident that the frightened wild creature was, at that moment in time, the most important thing in the world to Chelsea.

Ben was completely and utterly dumbfounded by the change in this woman. He had thought her unfeeling and cold. However, seeing her now, he realized that she might purposefully hold her emotions in check, but she definitely was not unfeeling. The deep concern and gentle kindness etched in her features astounded him. And again he was overwhelmed by the difference in her.

"Help me, Ben," she said, her voice feather soft so as not to upset the owl.

"What can I do?" He emulated her hushed tone as he crossed the room.

Just then May came into the living room with a linen tea towel.

"Here, Chelsea," May said. "This is the closest I could come to lightweight fabric."

"It's perfect," Chelsea said. "Thanks." Then she glanced at Ben. "Take the towel," she told him, "and loosely tie it over his head. Sort of like a hood."

"Over his head?" he asked.

"At least over his eyes," she instructed. "If he can't see, he'll stay calmer. But not too tight. We want him to be able to breathe."

Ben did as he was told, Chelsea quietly talking him through every movement. He marveled at how placid the bird had become when the makeshift hood was covering its head.

"I heard you scream," Ben said.

The sound of her chuckle made his gut tighten with pleasure.

"It was my fault. This little fellow scared me to death when he came down on top of me." She laughed softly again. "I should never have had my head in the hearth when you forced him down."

She held the bird in both hands and softly stroked it with one thumb.

"You're so scared," she crooned to the tiny owl. "It's going to be okay now."

Chelsea looked at Ben. "He's trembling," she said. Her eyes conveyed a tremendous amount of compassion. "Would you take me over to the nature center?"

"Sure."

"I'd go alone, but if I put him in a box I'm afraid he might hurt himself. It'd be safer for him if I just held on to him." She rubbed her chin on the owl's soft feathers. "I'd like to have the vet take a look at him.

He may have a broken wing, and if he does, I'm not sure how to set it."

"We can go right now," Ben said.

"Chelsea, you did an outstanding job." May's eyes were shining. "You sure did."

"I'm glad you called me," she said. "Let's go, Ben."

They drove the short distance to the nature center. By now the center was open and Chelsea went inside to hand over the bird to the attendant on duty.

As Ben waited for his wife to return to the truck, he went over what he'd learned about her. As long as he'd known Chelsea, she'd presented a reserved and chilly disposition to the world. And she'd been so consistent in her presentation that everyone believed her act.

But seeing her at May's this morning, actually witnessing the compassion she lavishly bestowed on the tiny, frightened owl, had taught him that his wife's detached demeanor was a facade—a false front that hid the true person inside. His wife definitely had an altruistic nature that she was concealing from him and everyone else around her.

The question that kept popping into his mind was: Why? What had happened to make her want to hide the true Chelsea from the world? Ben couldn't fathom what would compel a person to shut down her emotions—what would push her to stifle what most human beings reveled in. As he sat there with his elbow resting on the steering wheel, his chin tucked into the vee between his thumb and index finger, Ben decided that he was damned determined to find out.

* * *

Chelsea stood at the counter in Ben's kitchen, layering thin slices of baked ham onto chewy rye bread. The euphoria of having saved the helpless trapped owl still had her feeling as though she were floating on air. Even Ben's request that they spend the afternoon together sharing a picnic lunch hadn't popped her bubble of happiness, although it should have.

She couldn't help feeling a bit betrayed by Ben. She had expected him to fulfill his end of their deal without all this hoopla about "getting to know one another."

That first night, she'd fumed into the wee hours of the morning. How dare he suddenly decide to demand stipulations to a deal that had already been made, she had railed in the silence of her room. But then she'd mulled over his arguments in her head, and she'd had to admit that he did have a point.

It really wasn't fair of her to expect him to engage in a most intimate act with her, when she wasn't willing to cooperate. Her face heated at the mere thought.

The idea of being a participant in the act of sex was so alien to her. She'd never in her life imagined herself as part of a man/woman relationship. Why would she, when she knew she wasn't pretty enough, or good enough, or lovable enough to warrant a man's attention? Hadn't she been told again and again and again just how worthless she was? And hadn't she learned that each and every time she had tried to gain the affection of someone important to her, she had been slapped down and trampled on?

For the past few days she'd been worrying about Ben's insistence that the two of them become acquainted. She didn't want Ben to know her—didn't want to know him any more than she did right now. The distance between them, even though they were husband and wife, was safe for her. She was terrified to come any closer.

Ben was a nice person, a wonderful man. But if she opened up her emotions to him, she knew his inevitable negative reaction to what was revealed would hurt her, and she had to protect herself. It was imperative.

But she knew he'd made up his mind not to sleep with her until they had spent time together. So somehow she was going to have to get to know Ben, and at the same time disclose as little about herself as possible. The problem was complicated, and she hoped that she could manage to meet Ben's demands without making herself vulnerable to him.

"I found a blanket we can use."

Chelsea turned and saw Ben come into the kitchen.

"I thought we could have our picnic out in the Old Orchard," he said.

She nodded, then turned back to begin wrapping the sandwiches. Ben pulled a basket from the pantry and loaded it with fruit, napkins, a couple cans of soda. When she'd finished with the sandwiches, she tucked them inside with the rest of the food.

The Old Orchard was only a few hundred feet behind Ben's brick house. Here were the last of the original giant apple trees, the thick branches knurled, the bark rough and dark with age.

"Why do you keep them?" Chelsea asked.

Ben shrugged. "Granddad always said he kept them for sentimental reasons. I guess I feel the same. The dwarf trees are so much easier to prune and harvest, they're more economical. But these old trees remind me of what the orchard was like when I was a kid."

He stopped under one tree and spread out the blanket.

"I used to climb these trees," he said. "I want these trees to be around so my kids can climb them."

It was as though a jolt of lightning had zapped Chelsea and her gaze flew to Ben.

Immediately he looked contrite.

"I'm sorry," he said. "I didn't mean to...I wasn't thinking...I..." He shook his head and simply looked away from her.

Soon he turned to face her, his green eyes solemn, and he promised, "I'll try to be more aware of what I'm saying."

It was as though a gray cloud had moved over them, dimming the cheerful friendliness that had been between them only a second before.

What had compelled him to make that comment about his kids climbing in these trees? she wondered. Was he thinking of going back on his promise to give up his parental rights? No, she finally decided, Ben's an honorable man. It had simply been an offhand comment.

"These trees still bear fruit," he said, trying to ease the awkwardness. "It's just a pain to get at the apples."

Chelsea glanced up into the high branches and tried to imagine what it was like to climb the tall ladders necessary for harvesting the fruit.

"Here," Ben said, "sit down and let's have something to eat."

There was something in his voice that made her wary. She busied herself pulling food from the basket and fought to control the panic that was building inside her. She knew he'd brought her out here to talk. He'd want her to tell him all about herself.

She handed him a sandwich and forced her lips to curl into a smile. But she could feel the tightness around her mouth.

Maybe if she kept him busy talking about *his* family, about *his* childhood, then she wouldn't have to do much talking herself.

"Ben," she began, her voice tentative. "Tell me what it was like growing up at Reed's Orchard."

"Well, between May and Granddad, I had a lot of love," he told her. "Growing up on a farm, there were plenty of chores to do. But I played as hard as I worked."

She easily imagined him running in the sunshine and the fresh air. Most of the apartments and row homes where she'd spent most of her childhood didn't have yards, so she'd spent a great deal of time indoors. Chelsea shook the thought from her mind.

"When I was a baby, my parents and I lived in a house not too far from Aunt May's," Ben said.

At the mention of Ben's parents, Chelsea swallowed the bite of sandwich without even tasting the sweet baked ham. It wasn't that she didn't want to hear about his childhood, but she was scared to death that he might ask her about her own parents.

Ben didn't seem to notice her alarm. In fact, his gaze was trained on the horizon and his voice took on a wistful quality as he continued, "Apparently my father was something of a daredevil. My mom and dad were high school sweethearts and they married as soon as they earned their diplomas. My dad came to work for my grandfather, but Mom told me stories of how he was always getting into mischief."

He was involved with telling his story and Chelsea found her eyes traveling the length of his strong jawline. She liked the way his green eyes twinkled when he smiled, and she liked his straight, narrow nose. She found his features exceptionally pleasing. She hoped their baby would resemble him.

"My dad was fooling around one day on one of Granddad's tractors," Ben said. "He drove it up an incline that was too steep and the tractor rolled over. Dad didn't survive the accident."

"Oh, Ben," she said, sympathy welling inside her. "I'm so sorry." The words escaped before she even realized it.

"I was just a few weeks old, so I don't remember him at all." Ben inhaled and turned his gaze on her. "But my mom kept lots of pictures and she told me all about him. I know they loved each other very much. I feel like I know him." He flushed a little. "I guess that sounds silly to you."

"No," she said, her tone edgy. She turned away, uncomfortable with the emotion that threatened to be exposed.

"So tell me about your—"

"Your mom?" Her question cut him off with a terseness that bordered on rude, but she had anticipated his request about her past and asking about his mother had been her attempt to steer the conversation back on to him. It worked.

"Oh, my mom was beautiful," he said. "I remember a quick smile and a melodic voice that willingly sang lullabies and funny little ditties any time I asked."

Chelsea's heart ached at the picture he painted. It was so like the fantasies she'd conjured as a child.

Ben closed his eyes. "Her hair was the color of summer sunshine. And she had a dimple in one cheek. When she held me and smiled, I remember I would reach out and touch it."

When Ben looked at her again, his eyes had misted over and Chelsea's mouth went dry. She couldn't handle all this heartbreaking poignancy—she didn't know how to comfort herself, let alone anyone else. But then Ben smiled at her, and Chelsea knew it was meant to reassure her.

"My mother died when I was seven," Ben said. "Leukemia."

Again, sympathy surged through her. But this time it was not only for him.

"Seven must be the magic age," she murmured helplessly.

"What do you mean?"

She just shook her head, unable to speak around the lump that had suddenly risen in her throat.

Ben frowned. He could see that Chelsea was fighting back some sort of demon from her past—a demon she wasn't yet ready to reveal. He decided the best thing for him to do was to continue his verbal reverie and give her time to compose herself.

"Granddad took me in," he told her. "He and Aunt May loved me just as much as any parents would have. Life sometimes delivers some hard blows, but I've survived pretty well."

"Surviving is what counts," Chelsea commented in a tight voice.

Ben's eyes narrowed on her and he looked as though he was going to ask her to explain her statement, so she rushed to ask "How about school?" in an effort to turn the topic to something a little less emotional.

Ben grinned and reached up to run his fingers through his hair. "Oh, high school was great," he said. "I played football, ran on the cross-country team. I even joined the debate club."

"I'm impressed."

"But I wasn't quite ready for college."

"Oh?"

He shook his head. "I goofed off the first year. Almost flunked out. But Granddad succeeded in turning me around."

"And how did he do that?" she asked.

"He put me in charge of the books," Ben said wryly. "He put me in what is now your office and closed the door. The lesson was that it takes more than muscle to run a successful business." He chuckled. "I didn't have the first idea of what I was doing. But his plan worked. I went back to school the next fall with a deep commitment to learn something."

"That must have been when I came to work for your grandfather," Chelsea said. "John Reed hired me to straighten out the mess you made."

"He did, did he?" His emerald eyes danced. "And at which college, might I ask, did you learn to be such a wonderful accountant?"

"Oh, I didn't go to college," she said. "I was always good with numbers. I convinced John Reed of that and he gave me my first job."

Ben whistled his surprise. "Granddad hired you to keep his books and you had no college degree, no previous experience? Now *I'm* impressed. You must have given one hell of an inspiring talk."

Her chin dipped toward the ground. "I guess I did," she murmured.

She didn't want to reveal the terrible circumstances under which John Reed had hired her. Chelsea knew she owed the old man a lot, and that meeting him had been a turning point in her life. But she refused to confide those things in Ben.

Plucking at the blanket, she searched her brain for another question to ask him.

"Chelsea." His fingers touched her chin and gently lifted until their gazes met. "Tell me something about yourself."

When she didn't respond immediately, he tilted his head to the side and his eyes became persuasive.

"Tell me whatever you want," he coaxed. "Happy times. Sad times. Bad times. Good times. It doesn't matter. I just want to learn something about you."

She was helpless against the tortured expression that crossed her face. "Oh, Ben, please don't."

His hand remained on her cheek as he looked into her eyes. Finally, he said, "Well, we've made *some* progress anyway."

There must have been a question in her eyes because, with the tiniest of smiles at his lips, he went on to explain, "At least you trust me enough to let me know there's something you *don't* want to talk about."

No, Chelsea thought, *that's not true. I don't trust you. I can't.* But she hit a solid wall of confusion when she tried to figure out if she should believe his statement or her own thought.

"Everything will be okay."

His gentle tone did crazy things to her insides. So many times in her life she'd wanted someone to say those very words to her.

"If you don't want to talk yet, it's okay."

Again, her heart constricted at his words. It had been so long since anyone had treated her with such genuine concern and understanding.

His grin was boyish and charming. "Just you wait," he said. "Before long, you'll be telling me all about yourself and we'll be fast friends."

Chelsea could only stare at him and wonder if what he'd said would ever come true.

Chapter Five

When the column of numbers blurred together for the third time, Chelsea dropped her pencil in disgust and rubbed her eyes. It was no use. She couldn't concentrate on tabulating this week's debits. Not when her life was in such a topsy-turvy state.

She'd thought that by marrying Ben she'd solve all her problems and achieve her highest goal. But all she'd succeeded in doing was eroding the once-impenetrable wall that had taken years for her to build around herself.

That the wall was eroding she had no doubt, and Ben was the one at fault. He was forcing her to tear down, brick by brick, the safe fortress in which she'd once secured her emotions. She'd tried hard to wear down his resolve over the past couple of weeks, but Ben was adamant in his refusal to father her child until she completely demolished her reserved nature—her mighty castle—and confided in him all the secrets concerning her dark past.

Granted, he didn't realize just how painful her childhood memories were for her. He didn't know that she'd spent her whole life trying to suppress the hurt and loneliness she'd experienced as a little girl.

Chelsea gazed off into the far corner of her office. She supposed she could lie about her past. A happy, carefree childhood would be quite easy to fabricate—Lord knows how often she'd indulged in such fantasies when she'd been a young girl. But lying wouldn't be right. Not only wouldn't it be right, but it wouldn't be fair to Ben.

She'd come to realize what Ben meant when he'd said it wasn't fair for her to experience him at his most intimate, when she wasn't willing to reveal her innermost emotions to him.

She shook her head dismally. It all sounded so complicated. Because it was. And that's exactly why she had worked so hard all her adult life to maintain an emotional distance from people. Emotions were complicated things—hurtful, painful, distressing.

When she'd first offered Ben this deal, she'd thought everything would be simple and clear-cut. But now she understood that she had been stupid ever to think that a relationship with Ben would be simple.

It was impossible to deny that what they shared was anything other than a relationship. She had *tried* to remain distanced from him—to tell herself that what they shared was a business deal only. But they were living in the same house, eating the same meals, sharing in dozens of mundane tasks. It was inevitable that the two of them would develop some kind of relationship—it had been silly of her to think otherwise.

After spending so much time with Ben, she had begun to wonder how he actually felt about what she was asking him to do. Her request *must* mean more to him than simply a few passion-filled nights. In giving her a child, Ben would be giving her a part of himself.

Chelsea heaved a terrific sigh. How could she not have understood the magnitude of what she was asking of Ben? How could she have been so callous about the idea of his fathering her child?

Well, she might not have realized before, but she did now. She wanted a child badly, and she needed to make Ben comfortable with the idea of giving her that child. If that meant she would have to expose her vulnerable emotions to him, then she would do it.

She knew very well that in revealing herself she would be leaving herself open to any pain he chose to inflict. But that couldn't be helped. In order to get what she wanted from Ben, she'd have to give him the intimacy he required. She'd simply have to trust him not to hurt her.

Swallowing around the lump of fear that suddenly constricted her throat, Chelsea hoped she wasn't making the worst mistake of her life.

A dusky pink glow covered the evening sky when Ben finally arrived home from his work in the orchard. Chelsea had already eaten dinner and now sat on the front-porch step waiting for him.

"Hi," he said, closing the door to the truck.

"Hi." She tried to smile, but the anxiety she felt seemed to have frozen her facial muscles.

"What are you doing out here?" he asked.

"Waiting for you." And before he could inquire as to why, she said, "Are you hungry? Can I get you some dinner?"

He nodded, his eyes gleaming with unspoken appreciation. "I'm starved."

Ben offered her his hand. After a moment's hesitation she took it, and he pulled her to her feet.

They went inside and Chelsea busied herself fixing Ben a plate.

"What's wrong?"

She jumped when she realized he'd come up behind her.

"Nothing," she answered quickly.

"Come on, Chels." He took the plate from her hands, set it on the counter and turned her around to face him.

"It's not like you to be waiting for me at the front door," he said.

She lowered her gaze to the shiny floor tiles.

"What is it?" he asked.

It took all the strength she had to lift her gaze to his. Curiosity was clearly written on his face. She took a deep breath.

"I want to talk," she said. "I think it's time..." Her voice faltered, then she began again. "I think it's time that I told you why I want a baby."

Ben looked at her for a long, silent moment. It wouldn't have surprised her if he had hooted in triumph that she'd finally given in. At the very least, she'd expected a smile celebrating his conquest. But his reaction was not at all what she anticipated.

"Okay," he finally said, his eyes never losing their serious reflection. "Let me shower and change, and we'll talk."

After he'd left the room, Chelsea couldn't help feeling a little bewildered by his reaction. There had been no gloating; there hadn't even been a hint of strut in his step as he went toward his bedroom. His simple, calm demeanor soothed the nerves that jumped in her stomach. Ben was certainly a special person. She was discovering just how special with every new aspect of him that was revealed to her.

When Ben returned, he ate a quick dinner and then he and Chelsea went out onto the screened-in patio off the back of the house. They sat on the padded chaise longue and Ben turned his body so he was facing her.

Surprised by the calmness that had settled over her, Chelsea began her story, "I guess the best place to start is at the beginning."

She watched as Ben eased back and relaxed. His serene repose conjured an atmosphere of warmth and trust the likes of which she'd never before experienced. She didn't dare stop to question it—she simply continued with what she knew she must tell him.

"I don't have too many memories of growing up." Lifting one shoulder a fraction, she added with a murmur, "I guess the human brain has a terrific ability to repress . . . or forget. Whichever is needed."

She looked over his shoulder through the screened-in patio at the sky; the mauve shades of evening had given way to full-fledged darkness.

"My very first memories are of being in my bed," she said. "It was dark and I was afraid . . . no, I was terrified of the snakes."

"Snakes?"

Ben's question compelled her to look at him.

She paused a moment before explaining. "My mother wanted to go out at night, you see. She told me not to get out of bed or the snakes would bite me."

"Dear God!"

"And I wasn't to cry because I might wake them up."

The light from the kitchen dimly illuminated the patio, and Ben closely watched Chelsea's face. He couldn't believe what he was hearing. How could a mother do something so evil to her child?

"You were alone? Didn't she have someone to watch you? Why didn't she have a sitter? Your grandparents, or a neighbor?" His questions tumbled out one on top of the other.

Chelsea gave a mournful sigh and shrugged.

"Where was your father?" he asked and immediately felt a deep regret at the pain his query caused Chelsea.

"I never knew my father," she admitted meekly, as though this fact was somehow her fault.

Guilt consumed Ben. He shouldn't have asked all those questions. Especially the one concerning her father. And how could a child know that she shouldn't be home alone? What could Chelsea have done to help herself when she didn't know any different? When she didn't even know her mother's actions were irresponsible?

"Then one night I just couldn't control myself any more. And I cried."

He saw her eyes become hazy, as though she were telling her story to an empty room. Ben wouldn't force her to look at him, he felt bad enough because he was making her relive this horrible memory.

"I must have become awfully loud. The lady in the apartment next to us called the police. They came to the door." Her eyes grew large. "I was scared to death. I didn't dare get out of bed to answer the bell. The manager of the building unlocked the door to our apartment. Men came bursting in. I started screaming, trying to warn them about the snakes, but they wouldn't listen."

As he watched the tears well and spill over onto his wife's cheeks, Ben tried to imagine the terror she must have felt at that moment. He became overwhelmed with tender emotion for the little girl Chelsea described.

"My mother was so angry with me because she had to come and pick me up at some big brick building in Center City," she said. "I guess it was some kind of children's shelter. After that, she took me with her at night. But I was just as scared. I'd sit in the back seat of the car with all the doors locked. I'd cover my head with my blanket. I was so afraid someone would come and try to get me."

Ben could only shake his head in utter disbelief that a woman could treat a child so callously.

"I remember the last time she took me out in the car. I woke up and it was just getting light outside. I was hungry and thirsty. I had to go to the bathroom so badly... but I waited for my mother.''

He saw her throat move in a difficult swallow.

''But she never came. A man tapped on the window and tried to get in, but I wouldn't unlock the door. A lady from the police station came.''

Chelsea chuckled, but there was no hint of humor in her tone.

''But I still wouldn't let them in. They ended up using some kind of tool to unlock the car. I was crying for my mother. But she never heard me... she never came.''

Another tear slipped down her cheek.

''I don't remember much after that. I do know that I only saw my mother one last time.''

She sniffed and Ben reached over, pulled a tissue from the box and tucked it into her lifeless fingers. She made no move to dry her eyes.

''I remember sitting at this long table. There were lots of people there. Men in suits. Big briefcases. And a pretty lady in a flowered dress who kept smiling at me.''

Ben wanted to take Chelsea's hand, but didn't know if he should.

''My mother came into the room. She got very loud. Yelling and angry. Her face was all... red and ugly. Her eyes bulged and...''

Her voice went limp and then she seemed to let go of that particular memory.

''They finally took her out. Two policeman helped her out the door. Then all the people at the table talked.'' Her head tilted to one side. ''Their voices were low. I couldn't make out what they were saying. But...every once in a while the pretty lady would smile at me."

His gut tightened as he listened to Chelsea describe what had obviously been a hearing of a child-protection agency.

"I went to live with other children who had been taken from their homes."

Ben was helpless against his grunt of approval. "That's the best thing that could have happened," he murmured.

"But, Ben," she said, "it killed me to go there. I loved my mother. I cried for her every day. It felt like my heart had been ripped right out of my chest."

A lump rose in Ben's throat, and he didn't trust himself to respond. The child Chelsea had been couldn't have realized that she was being neglected, couldn't have known that the "men in suits" were only trying to protect her best interests.

"The people there—I called them nurses because they wore white uniforms—they were nice. For the most part."

She absently reached up, and in what looked like an almost childish gesture, she took a lock of her hair and began twirling it around her index finger.

"There was this one lady, though. She didn't like the kids much. I heard her talking about me. 'That Chelsea Carson, now there's a child only a mother could love, and hers doesn't.'" Chelsea's voice became thoughtful as she said, "It took me a long time to figure out what she meant."

Tucking the strand of hair behind her ear, she shook her head, almost as though she was physically putting the thought behind her.

"I went to live with a foster family after that." Her mouth pulled back into a sad, little smile and she whispered, "Mama Higgins."

Chelsea went silent for a long while and Ben willingly gave her all the time she needed.

Finally, she licked at her lips and continued. "I stayed with Mama Higgins—she asked me if I minded calling her that—for, oh, about a year, I guess."

She placed her fingers over her broadening smile. "I was very happy there," she said, lowering her hand. "I had new clothes, and I was never hungry. Mama Higgins let me help her cook dinner. We chopped vegetables. And I set the table." Her eyes twinkled in the dim light of the patio. "Christmas was wonderful that year. Santa actually brought me presents. I remember unwrapping this beautiful, curly-haired doll." She closed her eyes and nodded. "I was happy with Mama Higgins."

Then the fleeting joy that had brightened her features was suddenly gone and she sighed. "Then one day this social worker came. The lady told me that Mama Higgins wanted to adopt me. I didn't know exactly what that meant, I only knew it made me very happy. But the lady said that my mother refused to sign away her parental rights, and that I couldn't live with Mama Higgins any more."

"But, why?" Ben's zealous tone surprised him, and he calmed himself before he said, "The woman obviously wanted you. Why wouldn't the state let you stay there?"

Chelsea shrugged. "I don't know. Some state restriction. Some law maybe? Who can say?"

Ben couldn't believe the anger he felt. It was frustrating, because he wanted to yell at someone, take up for the lonely little girl who couldn't look out for herself. He wanted to make things right, but all this had happened so long ago.

"I was so young," Chelsea said. "But I knew that I never wanted to love anyone ever again. I learned that loving meant hurting. And I didn't want to hurt any more."

She grew quiet. It didn't take a genius to figure out that the terrible circumstances his wife had lived through had caused her heart to freeze. Ben resisted the urge to reach out and caress her cheek. He felt she might not appreciate the gesture, or worse, she just might resent it.

He was filled with so many emotions he had a hard time sorting through them all. Two things kept coming to the forefront of his mind. One was a fact: Chelsea's heart and soul were locked up tight. The other was a question: What could he do to release her, so that she could understand that joy was as much a part of life as the pain she had already experienced?

Chelsea felt drained. She harbored a deep sense of shame because of her childhood. If she wanted to be totally honest with Ben, she'd have to admit to him there was something wrong with her. She'd figured that out a very long time ago. Otherwise, why hadn't her mother loved her? Why had her mother given her away... like she had been some worn, out-of-fashion coat?

Yes, Chelsea knew she was very definitely flawed. Her mother hadn't loved her, and Mama Higgins hadn't been allowed to. But then, Ben already knew she was imperfect. How could he not? Saying the words aloud would only embarrass them both.

What she needed to do was finish her story and get this painful but necessary exposure out of the way.

"As soon as I was old enough," she said, her voice stronger now, "I left Philadelphia. I traveled around a bit. Worked odd jobs. And then one day I found myself in Kemblesville, right in the middle of Reed's Orchard."

She laughed softly. "John Reed was a crotchety old guy."

"That's true enough," Ben agreed.

"It was late fall and I was picking apples." Chelsea snorted, and then admitted, "Stealing them, actually. He caught me red-handed. I thought for sure he'd call the police. Have me arrested. But he didn't. He offered me dinner instead." She shook her head. "I was too surprised to decline."

Her mouth pulled into a wry grin. "He made me take a bath before he'd let me sit at his table. And then he told me I'd be doing some chores around the place to pay him back for his fruit."

"Ha!" Ben laughed. "That's my grandfather all right. Always telling other people what they'll be doing."

"I was belligerent toward him," she said, regretfully. "I was certain he'd turn his back on me sooner or later. But I've been here ever since."

She gazed at Ben. "So when you said I must have talked a good story to get the job, you were wrong. John Reed gave me this job because he knew I needed it. He knew without my telling him." In a far-off voice she added, "I hadn't realized that until just this moment."

"Chels, there's something I need to say." Ben cleared his throat before continuing. This was something he'd wanted to explain for a long time, but he never could figure out how to bring it up. "The winter I came home from college and you were working here... I just want to let you know how sorry I am about... what happened between us."

She went utterly still, and Ben hurried on with his own confession. "What I mean to say is... I never knew about all the things that you'd gone through. If I had, I never would have tormented you the way I did." He rubbed the back of his head with his hand. "Hell, I should admit it—I was just plain stupid. Whether I knew about your past or not has nothing to do with it."

The intensity was evident in her big, dark eyes, despite the shadows of the patio. Ben could only hope that she'd accept his apology.

"It's okay, Ben," she said.

"It isn't okay! It wasn't then and it isn't now. No one deserves to be treated the way I treated you." *Or the way others have treated you,* Ben thought.

"I shouldn't have let my friends rib me into coming on to you. Peer pressure is an awful thing." He made a disgusted sound. "Who am I kidding? It was my fault. I have to take responsibility for my own actions. I would have taken you out on a date—if you had taken me up on my offer."

Chelsea only looked at him. *Sure you would have,* she thought. *And I'm the queen of England, too.*

"I shouldn't have kept on and on about it," he said. "After you turned me down once, I should have left you alone. But I'd been drinking and I just didn't...I didn't..."

The deep regret expressed in his eyes touched her.

"If it's any consolation to you," he said in a humble tone, "my cheek smarted for three days."

Chelsea had to chuckle. "I am sorry I slapped you."

"I don't want you to apologize. I deserved it. I need for you to accept my apology."

"Look, it meant nothing. Okay?"

Ben saw her turn away from him. She was probably right. It *had* meant nothing to her. Chelsea had, in all likelihood, pushed the memory of what he'd done to her right out of her head. She'd filed it in her mind with all those other awful memories that needed forgetting. He felt horrible knowing that he had added to her pain.

"The reason we came out here," she said, intent on getting back to their original topic, "was so that I could try to make you understand why...why having a baby is so important to me. We've somehow wandered off track."

"That was my fault."

"Anyway..." Chelsea tucked her bottom lip between her teeth and wondered how she could make him understand her heart's desire. She couldn't possibly tell him it was because a baby would love her when no one else did. No, she had to explain her need to give.

"I want a baby," she began, "because I want to give my child a happy, carefree upbringing." That was certainly true enough. "I've always felt that some part of me was missing. I want to give my child...love." Those things, too, were true. But they sounded so pitiful to her ears. *Did Ben think so too?* she wondered.

Ben's heart ached for Chelsea. He could understand her desire to give a child all the things that she hadn't received. She had years and years worth of love to give—love that she'd pent up inside her—love she'd refused to let escape. If she were to have a child, she would finally be whole. And the thought of helping her to become complete filled him with euphoria.

"Ben, I—"

"Chels." He cut her off with a gentle voice. "I understand why you want a baby. I'd have to be a fool not to."

She looked at him and gave him a smile—the first one she'd given him that she didn't have to work at.

"You don't have to explain any more," he said.

The empathy in his eyes took her breath away. *He understands. He really understands.* She could see it on his face. Chelsea reached over and took his hand. And the ice that had encased her heart for so long began to chip away.

When he pulled her close, she didn't stiffen, she didn't feel impelled to resist. His arms were strong and his embrace was warm and secure. Chelsea relaxed into it, and for the first time since speaking her marriage vows, she thought that maybe everything *was* going to be okay.

Ben leaned close and she could feel his breath on her ear. Ever so softly, he whispered, "Let's go make a baby."

Chelsea tingled all over and felt her heart turn over in her chest. "You mean it?" she asked. "Right now? Tonight?"

His glittering eyes reflected the excitement and anticipation she knew radiated from her.

He nodded. "Right now. Tonight."

"Oh, Ben," she said, feeling close to tears. "Thank you so—"

Placing two fingers against her lips, he shook his head. "Don't," he told her.

His gentle timbre and the promise of unselfish giving that lit his emerald gaze melted the last remnants of frost that coated her heart. She felt emotionally naked, totally exposed to Ben. And although the feeling was mysterious and new to her, she marveled at the fact that she hadn't the least bit of fear. It warmed her heart to know that he was doing everything he could to make her feel safe, and she appreciated that.

He traced the line of her jaw, the pads of his fingers sliding along ever so slowly. When her chin was tucked into the vee of his hand between his index finger and thumb, he lifted her jaw a fraction and forced her eyes to meet his.

With gazes locked, they communicated in silence. Tension built around them until it was nearly a tangible thing.

Slowly, the look in his eyes changed. The altruism dimmed and a flicker of heated passion took its place. The spark caught, and held, and grew. And it spread over his features until the desire he felt was etched in every plane and angle of his face.

A shiver ran up Chelsea's spine and she pressed her palm flat against her stomach when an unidentified, yet undeniable warmth began to curl there. Before she could wonder what was happening to her, Ben lowered his head and covered her mouth with his.

His kiss was like nothing she'd ever felt before. His lips, hot and moist against hers, performed a tender exploration. She closed her eyes and gave herself over to the intriguing sensations that bombarded her senses.

He opened his mouth and timidly ran the tip of his tongue across her bottom lip. She instinctively knew he was questioning her. How far did she want him to go?

She desperately wanted him to know that she understood his need to trust—that she intended to meet his need by giving herself as completely and totally as she was able.

Parting her lips, she welcomed his tongue with her own. She kissed him deeply, thoroughly, and hoped he would recognize this intimate, unspoken expression for what it was.

He did. And she knew it because his lips became bolder, more ardent in their pursuit. His tongue delved into her mouth, playing erotic games with hers that heated the curls of emotion in her stomach until they burned white-hot.

Finally, he pulled back a hair's breadth, kissing her mouth lightly, once, twice, three times.

She didn't move, or rather, was unable to. It seemed as though the oxygen in the air was thin and inadequate. Evidently, Ben felt the same way, because he filled his lungs deeply. As he exhaled, he gave her a broad smile.

"Let's go back to the bedroom," he suggested.

She could only nod.

Ben stood and pulled her to her feet. Entwining his fingers with hers, he led the way through the kitchen, down the hall and into his room.

The giddy excitement that jumped inside Chelsea had her shaking uncontrollably.

Ben stopped beside the bed, and obviously mistaking her trembling as fear, he said, "There's no reason to be afraid."

"Oh, I'm not afraid," she assured him.

"Good."

He seemed so pleased by her answer, and for some reason that made Chelsea very happy.

Ben reached up and loosened the top button of her blouse. She covered his fingers with her hand and waited until he looked into her eyes.

"I want you to know that . . . I'm going to try to enjoy myself," she said.

He grinned. "If you have to try, then I won't be doing my job."

"What I meant to say," she tried again to make him understand, "was ... that I never have ..."

His brows knit together. "You've never enjoyed yourself sexually? Well, I—"

She stopped him with an embarrassed and frantic shake of her head. "No, no. I'm trying to let you know that I've never ... I haven't ever ..."

It was no use. She couldn't bring herself to say the words out loud.

"You've never had sex?"

Ben's question was filled with a strange mixture of incredulity and wonder. He watched her closely, her averted gaze answering his question. This woman was an enigma to him. He kissed her gently on the mouth.

"It'll be okay," he promised.

She's never been touched. The words rang in his brain, and he was amazed by how erotic he found them. Hugging her to him, he felt her tremble and knew that he'd have to take things very slowly. He'd be the first man to touch her body. And after all the things he'd learned about her tonight, he hoped he'd be the first to touch her soul.

Chelsea's heart pounded in her chest as she stood in the circle of Ben's arms. When he stepped back and started to unbutton her blouse, she marveled at how her skin began to tingle with a heightened awareness. He pushed back the facings of her blouse and sucked in his breath. Pride welled inside her at the thought of causing such a reaction in him.

He slipped her blouse from her arms and let it fall unheeded to the floor. His warm hands slid up her arms and over her bare shoulders. He ran his little finger underneath the rose-colored lace of her bra, and her nipples tightened into buds that strained against the thin, satiny fabric. She heard herself gasp, saw his satisfied smile, and her heartbeat thumped even harder.

He took hold of her hand and raised it to his chest. Fingering the buttons of his shirt, she was overwhelmed with the unspoken knowledge of what he wanted of her. A flash of trepidation shot through her. Could she answer his silent request?

With tentative, fumbling fingers she began to undress him. She had trouble with one stubborn button, but it finally popped free. Her shaky hands tugged the shirt over his muscular shoulders and down his taut, well-defined arms.

Heat radiated off his skin, causing peculiar emotions to race through her. The warm, clean smell of him made her want to move closer and bury her nose in the crook of his neck.

He unclasped the front hook of her bra, and as it slid to the floor he bent over and kissed her shoulder. His tongue flicked out to taste her skin.

"You're so sweet." His voice was a husky whisper. "I want to taste you all over."

His eyes were filled with such passion that she felt a sudden urge to look away. Her gaze traveled over the curly hair that covered his broad chest. Curiosity got the best of her, and she reached out and splayed her hand there. The hair was springy and soft, and the feel of it sent jolts of heat shooting through her.

She stopped suddenly, her fingertips directly over his heart. It pounded just as furiously as her own. Her gaze flew to his and again she could clearly see his desire displayed in his hungry green eyes.

"Oh, Ben."

At that moment she lost her heart to him. The man made her feel so beautiful, so desirous, so...worthy.

Her voice dropped an octave and she repeated, "Oh, Ben."

The words must have called him to action, because without knowing how, Chelsea found herself lying on the bed, stripped of everything except the building desire that left her feeling flushed and wanting. Ben slipped out of his trousers and lay down beside her.

He touched, kissed, teased, tasted, tempted, until she felt she would suffocate from breathlessness.

During the few moments that she could think coherently, she touched and kissed and touched some more. His skin was smooth as satin, hot as flame. The sound of his moans nearly drove her mad. The silky spot on his inner wrist brushed the swell of her breast. He slid his hand over the valley of her waist, the curve of her hip. And his lips seemed to touch every inch of her. She felt as if she were climbing higher and higher, but she had no idea of where this journey was taking her.

This new and wild experience was more than just a physical adventure for her. Ben was conjuring emotions in her that she hadn't even known existed.

She felt that she and Ben were alone on some high, never-before-reached precipice. They danced to an erotic, primal rhythm that she vaguely recognized as her own heartbeat. He twirled her, they dipped, spun, whirled and swayed. Until finally they glided too close to the cliff's edge and she tumbled over into a silent void of pure carnal sensation.

Chapter Six

The metal file drawer closed with a clank, but Chelsea continued to clutch the handle as her thoughts flew like a flock of cawing crows. The past two weeks had been like nothing she'd ever imagined. The days had been brighter and sunnier than she'd ever known them to be. Ben had been so attentive to her.

And the nights!

The nights had been filled with physical pleasures beyond her wildest dreams. As a lover, Ben was extremely generous. Each night, he revealed a new secret about her body that she hadn't known existed—which areas of her flesh were ticklish, which craved to be touched. He seemed to delight in the knowledge that they were discovering her sexuality together.

During one instance when her inexperience had impelled her to become timid, Ben had calmed her fears and assured her that pleasure *should* be part of their sexual encounter. He'd patiently explained his desire for her to remember her baby's conception as a happy and satisfying event. Chelsea grinned, remembering the lascivious smile that had curled his lips when he'd realized his description held a double-edged meaning.

Because satisfied truly described how she felt after a night in Ben's arms. He made her feel more feminine than a woman had any right to feel. After they made love—she'd tried hard not to use that term to describe what they did together, but there was no other description that fit—Chelsea wanted to stretch like a satiated feline, curl into a ball tucked in his arms and fall asleep. But she hadn't let herself.

Absently, Chelsea reached around and rubbed the dull ache in the small of her back.

No, she'd been very careful to get out of Ben's bed and go to her own room. Night after night, she would slip between the cool, empty sheets of her lonely bed and spend hours trying to fall asleep.

That first night he had asked her to stay with him. But she'd insisted on sleeping in her own room. She knew very well that she did so in order to protect herself. It would be very easy to fall prey to the sensuous gratification she'd found in Ben's arms.

She *knew* the reason they were together was so she could become pregnant, and that there was nothing more to their lovemaking than that. But she was still amazed by what all this pure hedonistic pleasure did to her emotions. Her once rock-hard heart had become a soft and mushy place inside her. Her experience with Ben affected the way she saw the world.

Flowers looked more beautiful, trees appeared greener, the sky bluer, the clouds puffier. What frightened her the most was the fact that Ben had come to mean something more than he had before.

When she'd gone into this whole marriage deal, Ben had meant a father for her child—that and nothing more. But now...

She let the thought trail, too afraid to plant the seed, afraid the idea might sprout and grow. But it grew nevertheless.

Are you in love with Ben? The silent question floated through her mind, freezing icicles of fear inside her. Loving someone meant offering them the opportunity to cause her pain. She knew that. She was determined never to let it happen again.

You are not in love with Ben Danvers, she sternly answered the question. What she felt was lust. Pure, unadulterated lust. That she could allow herself to feel, and she'd simply have to learn to ignore the emptiness the word left in the pit of her stomach.

The knock on her door made her screeching thoughts fly into oblivion.

"Come in," she called.

A chuckling May pushed into the office.

"I just had to share this with someone." There was awe in May's voice, and she brandished a tabloid newspaper as if it were a proclamation from the president himself. "Ready?" she asked, then continued without waiting for Chelsea's reply, "'Baby Born with Gold-capped Tooth.'"

Chelsea's brows pulled into a slight frown. "But, May, babies are born toothless."

"Not this one," May replied emphatically. "This article tells about a baby who was born with a full set of thirty-two teeth. And not only that, but one of those teeth was covered with a twenty-four-karat gold cap."

Chelsea forced herself not to smile at May's apparent gullibility.

"Maybe you shouldn't believe everything you read," she gently suggested. "I mean, have you ever known anyone in Kemblesville to give birth to a baby who already had a full set of teeth?"

May looked at her a moment, her eyes glassy as she thought about the question.

Finally, the older woman said, "Well, now that you mention it, no, I haven't. But I read in the paper about a woman who accidently swallowed a penny while she was pregnant, and when the baby was born it was clutching a penny in its fist."

Chelsea couldn't hold back her laughter this time. "Oh, May, I'm afraid you're hopelessly trusting."

"Oh, speaking of trusting," May said, "I wanted to let you know that a lady from the nature center came and released the owl."

Nodding, Chelsea said, "I know that they kept the little fellow for a couple of days. His feathers had to be cleaned. But he was okay."

"Do you think he might have trouble with my chimney again?"

"He shouldn't," Chelsea said. "Owls are pretty smart."

"I worried that maybe he should have been taken somewhere else and let go." May raised one shoulder. "Maybe deeper into the woods or something?"

"Most likely he lives in a tree near your house," Chelsea explained. "It's the center's policy to release wild animals as close as possible to the place they were found." Suddenly, she inhaled slowly and rubbed at her cramping stomach.

"Are you okay?" May asked.

"Actually, I'm not feeling very well." Chelsea smoothed her fingers across her forehead. "I have a headache and my stomach hurts a little. Not to mention my back."

"Why don't you go on home?" May suggested. "I'm sure you don't have anything to do that can't wait until tomorrow. Go home and lie down. I'll answer your phone."

Chelsea nodded. "I think I'll take you up on your offer."

When she walked into Ben's house, she felt worse than ever. Her skin tingled all over and there was a tension in her stomach she couldn't define. Her head pounded and she wondered if she was coming down with some sort of flu.

She passed by her bedroom door, knowing perfectly well she should have gone in there to lie down. But something seemed to pull her toward Ben's room, and she crawled across his big, soft mattress and tried to relax.

The male scent that was Ben's alone clung to his pillow and she hugged it to her. She felt so achy all over, she didn't want to think about why the smell of him gave her such comfort or why being in his bed made her feel so close to him in his absence.

Why did she feel the need to be close to him simply because she felt ill? It was silly. Her brain just wasn't working right because of this flu or whatever was wrong with her.

Questions danced at the edges of her mind. What would Ben think if he came home and found her in his bed? How would he react to the sight of her clutching his pillow to her aching abdomen?

I'll get up in a minute, she promised herself. *I'll get up and go into my own room in just one moment.*

"Chelsea?"

Ben softly closed the front door behind him. Aunt May had told him Chelsea had gone home earlier in the day to lie down. He'd left the paperwork undone on his desk, the planned phone calls unmade, in order to answer an undeniable urge to check on her.

The setting sun cast mauve shadows in the house. Ben walked on light feet down the hall, so as not to disturb Chelsea if she were sleeping.

He peered around the corner of her bedroom door and frowned when he saw the empty bed. Going to his room, he looked through the crack left by the partially open door. Chelsea lay on the bed, her knees drawn up toward her chest.

A worried crease gathered between his eyes. She must have been terribly sick to have gotten into the wrong bed. Chelsea was very adamant about sleeping in her own room—so adamant, in fact, that he'd felt a bit affronted at first.

Meaning to go to her to check for fever, Ben pushed open the door of the room. The hinges creaked and Chelsea stirred.

"It's okay," he assured her.

"What time is it?" she asked, sliding to the edge of the bed. "I didn't mean to fall asleep."

"It's okay," he repeated. "Don't get up. I only came to check on you."

"I have to get up," she insisted. "I need to use the bathroom."

As she brushed past him, he reached out and touched her arm. He felt relieved that her skin didn't feel feverish.

Standing outside the closed bathroom door, he heard the toilet flush, the water run, and then he thought he heard her crying.

He knocked on the door. "Chelsea?"

When there was no answer, he knocked again. "Let me in, Chels."

She opened the door, and even in the darkened hallway he saw tears glistening in her eyes.

"What is it? What's wrong? Are you sick?"

His anxiety over her obvious distress made him ask his questions one on top of the other, giving her no time to answer.

Her bottom lip trembled and he grasped her upper arms.

"Please, Chels, tell me."

"I'm not pregnant."

WIFE FOR A WHILE

It only took him the span of one heartbeat to figure out what her simple, whispered statement meant. She'd started her menstruation cycle and she was disappointed that she hadn't conceived a child.

He didn't say anything. He only took her in his arms and held her to him tightly.

For some odd, unexplainable reason, he felt the smallest bit of pleasure that she hadn't yet become pregnant. But he hadn't time to even think about why before he was overwhelmed with a monstrous sense of guilt.

"I can't believe I feel so—" she cried softly against his shoulder "—let down."

"It's understandable," he said.

"I feel awful. All crampy and my back hurts."

Running his hand down the length of her arms, he suggested, "Why don't you take a quick shower and change into something comfortable?"

She nodded and went back into the bathroom.

He heard the shower running as he fixed them a quick sandwich and a simple salad.

By the time she padded out to the kitchen, her freshly washed hair braided down her back, he had set the table and was just placing food on the plates.

"Oh, Ben," she said. "Thanks so much, but I don't feel very hungry. I just want to go to bed."

"No problem," he told her. "I can wrap this up."

He went to the cabinet beside the sink. "Here, take these." After he handed over the two pain-relieving tablets, he filled a glass with water and offered it to her.

She swallowed one pill and then stopped to look at him. "You know, I should have seen this coming," she said. "I mean I've lived with this monthly curse for years now." She swallowed the other tablet. "Headache, backache, cramps. They show up every month, and I know what follows. I really should have seen this coming."

"Well," Ben said, "you've had other things on your mind lately."

Chelsea exhaled a quick, derisive breath. "You can say that again. I haven't thought of anything except getting pregnant. I'm afraid I'm becoming obsessed with the idea."

"Come on," he said.

As he lead her down the hallway, he couldn't help but feel a little hurt by what she'd said. The thought that she was so focused on the conception of a child somehow made him feel less... human. It somehow took away from the fact that he was a flesh-and-blood man. It was stupid of him to feel this way. He realized it wasn't her intention to devalue him in any way, but he felt it just the same.

She paused at his bedroom door. "Where are you taking me?"

"Well, that's a silly question," he said, guiding her on into his room. "You said that you had a backache," he said. "I can help with that. Lie on your stomach."

She did as he bid and lifted her weight to make it easier for him to pull her loose-fitting nightshirt up to her shoulders.

"My hands are a bit rough," he said by way of apology.

"There's a bottle of skin cream on my dresser." Her voice was muffled by the pillow.

When he got back with the lotion, he saw that her nightshirt was a rumpled heap on the floor by the bed. The sight of her slender naked back tied his gut in knots.

Ever since the first time he'd made love with Chelsea, he'd been awed—and continued to feel awed—by how sexually attractive he found her. The sight of her naked skin nearly drove him wild. The scent of her naked skin *did*.

He really hadn't expected to have such a strong reaction to her. Yes, she was pretty, what with her large dark eyes and long chestnut hair. Her cute button nose would catch the attention of any red-blooded male. But his reaction to her was far stronger than what he felt should be normal.

In fact, he was certain from the way he churned inside when he was near her, he'd have no trouble at all giving her as many babies as she wanted, and then some—

"Is something wrong?"

Chelsea lifted her head and twisted a fraction to look at him. His face grew hot with embarrassment over his thoughts. Averting his gaze from the visible swell of her breast, he hurried to the bed and sat on its edge.

"Let me just warm some of this up," he said, trying to control his flustered state. He poured a dollop of lotion into his palm and rubbed his hands together.

Just keep your mind on the job at hand, he silently told himself.

The task may have been small, but it took an enormous effort for him to focus on his goal. He smoothed his hands over her back to distribute the creamy lotion.

Her flawless skin felt like silk to his work-roughened hands. The milk white color was more than pleasing to his eyes, and he had to force himself to concentrate.

His fingertips ran over the tiny bumps of her spine as he slowly made his way down her back. He reversed the action and heard her sigh softly in response. That sigh sparked something deep inside him—a slow-growing flame that had never been completely extinguished during the past two weeks despite the satisfaction he found in their lovemaking.

With the heels of both hands, he pressed little circles on the indentations on either side of her spine at the small of her back.

"That's wonderful," she groaned.

Her avid reaction was like a sprinkling of water on a dry desert—he wanted more of it, much more.

Working mostly with his strong thumbs, he massaged his way up her back. He rubbed her shoulder muscles and was rewarded with a tiny moan. He smoothed his palm over her shoulders and heard her sigh.

Ben had to fight the urge to bend over and plant a tender kiss on her neck. The flame that had flickered inside his gut only a moment ago, now blazed with an ever-growing heat. Chelsea did this to him, and he couldn't figure out why.

He really needed to get his mind off the desire that gnawed at him, but that was nearly impossible when the object of his passion was laying on his bed half-naked.

Talk, he commanded himself.

"How is this?"

"Mmm," she answered, groggily.

He smiled and splayed his hands across her shoulder blades, kneading with strong fingers.

"I've heard several different terms used to describe the female monthly cycle," he said. "You may not believe it, but a couple of the married men who work for me talk quite freely concerning just about all aspects of their relationships with their wives. I've heard Joe complain that 'Angela is suffering from the curse this week.'" He chuckled. "Tom never fails to let everyone know 'Teresa is spitting fire.' Apparently she becomes very irritable."

Ben let his fingers trail lightly down Chelsea's back.

"I remember before Aunt May went through menopause she'd tell me, 'Don't bother me. I'm feeling out of sorts.'"

He saw that Chelsea's breathing had become relaxed and even, and a deep sense of satisfaction settled over him knowing that he might have helped relieve her discomfort.

With ever-lighter strokes, he worked his way up to her shoulder blades. When his fingertips accidentally brushed the soft swell of her breasts, the satisfaction he felt was quickly snuffed out by the white-hot fire of his need.

Damn, he admonished himself. How could he be so callous? He felt totally helpless against the reactions that his wife caused in him, but he certainly could control his urges while she was feeling "out of sorts." A faint grin crept across his lips.

He had to admit that he did feel the smallest bit pleased that Chelsea wasn't pregnant. His grin disappeared completely as the thought flashed through his brain. He wasn't proud that he felt that way, and he knew it was totally selfish, but he looked forward to making love to her. He enjoyed it. And their hot, fully satisfying nights of love would stop cold once she conceived.

Ben stopped massaging and leaned over to gaze at Chelsea's face. He was certain she was asleep. Reaching out, he brushed a strand of her shiny, dark hair from her face.

He picked up the baggy cotton shirt she used for pajamas and absently folded the lightweight material. All he asked, looking at the ceiling as though his gaze could somehow get his selfish prayer to heaven, was that it would take her a while to become pregnant.

Before Chelsea was fully conscious, she became aware of the heated male scent that belonged to Ben. She inhaled deeply and thought she must be dreaming.

But as she came awake, she frowned. Something wasn't right. She raised her lids and blinked her sleepy eyes several times.

Something was wrong. She was in Ben's room. In Ben's bed. In Ben's arms.

His deep, steady breathing was right next to her ear. His arm was tucked beneath her breasts. The two of them were pressed together like spoons in a cutlery drawer.

She lay as still as a frightened rabbit and tried to remember what had happened last night that had impelled her to sleep with Ben.

Slowly, images came to her. She'd come home early from work with a headache and body aches. She'd lain down on Ben's bed because for some reason she'd found comfort there. Ben had come home. He'd given her pain tablets. He'd given her...

The disappointment she'd experienced yesterday over not being pregnant was nothing next to the deep sense of gratitude she felt toward the man who lay sleeping beside her. No one had ever taken the time to care for her the way he had last evening. And she hadn't even been sick, really. She'd only been experiencing a completely natural, sometimes annoying monthly condition that every woman was forced to suffer at sometime in her life.

But Ben had treated her with kindness and understanding. And a tenderness she'd never before been shown. He'd even gone beyond that by giving her a massage that had alleviated her painful backache. Then he'd obviously curled up next to her so she wouldn't be alone in her misery.

She felt the warm weight of his forearm as it pressed so intimately up under her bare breasts. The tiny hairs on his arm tickled her sensitive skin. But it wasn't uncomfortable, in fact it was quite . . . delicious.

An inadvertent sigh escaped her lips—a sigh filled with utter satisfaction. She'd never slept all night with anyone. Inhaling deeply, she let the contentment wash over her. Being married to Ben had brought her some beautiful and fulfilling experiences—experiences she would treasure for the rest of her life.

She'd learned so much about him. His sexual drive was strong and his passion overwhelmed her. She also knew he was a kind man, an understanding man, a man who cared about others. He'd proven that last night. And he was a strong man, but his was a quiet strength . . . a quiet strength that awed her.

All these thoughts made her mouth go dry. Her stomach seized up with a sudden fear.

Easing from his cozy embrace, she slid to the edge of the mattress and sat up. Her nightshirt was folded at the foot of the bed, and she tugged it over her head. She stood and made her way to the door as she pushed her arms into the sleeves.

She stopped off at the bathroom and then went to the kitchen to fix a pot of coffee. She barely heard the steady *glub, glub* of the perking coffee as she gazed out the kitchen window. Trying desperately to focus on the predawn sky with its coral mother-of-pearl sheen, Chelsea couldn't stop the question from entering her brain.

Have you fallen in love with Ben?

Her fingertips felt chilled as she pressed them to her lips. She knew her feelings for him had mellowed from the very beginning, when he'd agreed to father her child. It had been impossible for her not to feel soft emotions, when he had been willing to give her the one thing she desired above all else.

And tenderness for him had invaded her further when he'd treated her so very gently as she'd explained her childhood to him.

He'd cared for her when she'd felt so awful, and she'd awakened in his strong arms. As she had lain there in his warm, protective embrace and she'd pondered all the things she'd learned of him, she'd become all tingly inside.

Have you fallen in love with Ben?

The question was relentless, and though silent, it seemed louder this time. Her subconscious, or whatever it was that was querying, was certainly demanding an answer.

But she couldn't fall in love with Ben. That hadn't been part of her original plan—her simple, clear-cut plan.

If she were to fall in love with him, she'd experience more pain than she'd ever encountered in her life. She couldn't let that happen. She just couldn't.

Even in her wildest imaginings, she couldn't picture Ben feeling affectionate toward her.

This is a child only a mother could love. This is a child only a mother could love. The social worker's words from years earlier swam through her mind, just as they had all her life.

No, Ben could never love her.

Have you fallen in love with Ben?

The question *was* louder this time, and it wasn't going away.

Chelsea's throat convulsed as she tried to swallow around the dryness in her mouth. Her chin trembled the slightest bit as she finally admitted, ''Yes.''

Chapter Seven

"May—" Chelsea's tone held the tentative note of someone unused to seeking out social conversation. "Tell me about your marriage."

The two women were sitting in Reed's Orchard Country Store. Chelsea loved the homey atmosphere, with the delicious aroma of apples permeating the air and the quaint country crafts and preserves for sale.

"Well, child," May began, "I was eighteen when I first laid eyes on Joshua Harris. He was a professor in a small seminary college in Philadelphia. He'd come to Kemblesville to our church one Sunday as a visiting preacher."

May worked at tatting a delicate lace doily, her nimble fingers maneuvering the small shuttle through the web of cotton thread until the series of knots formed an intricate and beautiful design. So skilled was she at the craft that her hands didn't slow, even though her eyes glazed with her happy reminiscences.

"I was carried away by his fiery words and his inspiring manner." She chuckled impishly. "His big, broad shoulders and handsome face didn't hurt much, either."

Chelsea's lips drew back humorously.

"We were introduced during the welcome hour after the service. That's the time that church members spent socializing—catching up on all the gossip."

May's rocking chair stopped its creaking, but her fingers continued to weave the wooden shuttle up and down, in and out. "Joshua became a regular member of our congregation after that. He traveled from the city to our small town every Sunday. After two short weeks, he went to my father. At first, my father flat refused to even consider Joshua's request to court me."

"Joshua asked to court you?" Chelsea couldn't contain her disbelief.

"Oh, yes," May said. "Joshua would never have pursued a relationship with me without my father's permission. Things were very different back then. My father would have brandished a shotgun in order to protect my virtue, if need be. It might have been against the law, but he'd have had the support of all his relatives, friends and neighbors. And Joshua knew it."

"It all sounds so... Victorian."

"It was," May agreed.

"But didn't you have any say in who—" Chelsea stumbled over how to say what she was thinking "—came courting?"

May shook her head. "Not until a formal request was made. Once Joshua had my father's permission, he could ask for mine."

Chelsea was intrigued by the devilish gleam in May's eye.

"I can't tell you the number of come-hither smiles and flirtatious looks I had to cast Joshua's way, in order to bolster him into continuing his petition."

Narrowing one eye, Chelsea commented, "I think you had more say about who came courting than you're letting on."

May grinned like a Cheshire cat. "Maybe so," she admitted. "If anyone had seen the way I enticed Joshua—" her eyes grew large and she shook her head "—I would have been called a brazen hussy."

Her light chortle echoed softly. "But he was worth the risk," May said, her voice growing hushed. "Oh, my, he was certainly worth the risk."

A silence settled over them as May continued tatting. Chelsea was disheartened by May's silence. She had been thoroughly enjoying this newfound pastime of hers; she'd never sought out someone simply to talk. She'd had to force herself to come in here and invoke this conversation with May. She was reluctant to let it lull and die away.

"So," she said, "your relationship with Joshua was special?"

May slowly nodded, her fingers once again growing still. "I enjoyed nearly ten wonderful years of marriage. Oh, we didn't have much. As a seminary professor, Joshua only made a pittance. And his salary as a visiting minister was spotty at best. But I planted a garden, and canned food for the winter. I made quilts and doilies and sold them. I took in some sewing. My father would have helped us out, but Joshua was such a proud man."

The gleam in May's eyes conveyed that she was pleased with that trait in her man.

"We were married on Christmas Eve. The happiest day of my life." Then May's voice fluctuated with heartfelt sadness as she added, "But then World War II came marching along. A day of infamy." The old woman sighed, her eyes growing misty. "Joshua was hell-bent on signing up, and he promptly became a casualty of war."

"Oh, May." Chelsea's own throat ached with the pain and loss that May had felt all those years ago— the pain and loss she obviously continued to feel.

"We almost made our tenth anniversary," May said. "But not quite." Suddenly she shook herself, as though physically removing the bad memories and setting them away from her.

She looked at Chelsea and smiled. "But I did enjoy the wonderful fortune of spending over nine wonderful years with the man I loved. Nine years that were a gift from above."

"A gift?"

May's gaze turned soft. "Chelsea, there is absolutely nothing that can compare to the relationship between a man and woman in love. Nothing."

She started her chair to rocking again. "I'm not talking about the physical aspects of marriage. Although that's wonderful, too." She let the cotton thread and shuttle drop into her lap and she paralleled her palms an inch apart in front of her. "When a person can actually touch the soul of another—" she pressed her hands together and closed her eyes "—become one with another human being." May shook her head and whispered, "There is nothing on this earth that can compare with that."

"You loved your husband a lot," Chelsea observed.

May only nodded.

"It's sad that you only had nine years..."

The older woman's face became serene as she said, "One moment in heaven is worth an eternity in hell."

Chelsea couldn't imagine developing that kind of relationship with someone. She'd come to the stark realization that she loved Ben, that she wanted to be with him, that she wished he felt... But there her thoughts had dwindled. These wants and wishes were so useless. Empty fantasies that could never be.

"But it takes more than just love."

May's comment drew Chelsea's attention.

"More?" Chelsea asked.

"It takes commitment..."

I could give Ben that, she thought.

"It takes loyalty..."

I could give him that, too.

"And it takes a great deal of trust."

Chelsea's shoulders sagged and she let her gaze lower to the floor. She swallowed and wondered if she could ever allow herself to give Ben her full and complete trust.

"But," May said, "no successful relationship is one-sided. It's a two-way street. Both individuals must be willing to give one hundred percent of the love, commitment, loyalty and trust it would take to make a relationship successful. One hundred percent. It won't work otherwise."

A deep sense of sadness washed over Chelsea at May's comments. No matter what she wanted to give to Ben, be it love, commitment, loyalty or even trust, she could never hope to share the kind of relationship with him that May was talking about. She could never "touch his soul," because he would never be willing to travel the two-way street with her. No, Ben had married her for the sole purpose of saving his orchard. And she had known that going into the marriage.

"I'll never have that." Chelsea hadn't meant to speak the words aloud.

"Of course you will," May said.

Chelsea looked at May and couldn't help but notice how sincere she seemed. May really appeared to care about the fact that Chelsea felt she'd never find the kind of life mate that May had found in her Joshua.

But why should May care about her? Chelsea had spent all of her years at Reed's Orchard working to keep everyone at arms' length. She had intentionally kept herself apart—purposefully kept herself from caring for others so others wouldn't care for her. No, she'd given May no reason to feel concern.

A forlorn little half smile cocked up the corner of Chelsea's mouth. "Trust me on this, May. I never will."

A deep depression settled over her like a heavy, stifling blanket, and she felt a sudden overwhelming need to get out into the open air, alone.

"May, it's nearly quitting time," Chelsea said. "My work's all done for today. I'm going to hike over to the nature center to see if there's anything that I can do."

"Okay," May said. "I'll let Ben know where you are."

Chelsea nodded. "Tell him I'll see him later at... home."

It was so hard for her to think and speak of Ben's house as her home. A home was supposed to be a place where a person could find love and security—a place where...

She let the thought glide right out of her mind, realizing that never in her life had she ever had a real home of her own.

Lord, she had to stop thinking this way, she was getting downright morbid.

Chelsea held the door open for a customer and then went outside and lifted her face to the late-afternoon sun. She started off toward the woods across the parking lot, hoping the long walk to the center could clear her doldrums. But she sincerely doubted it would work.

Her large plastic bag was less than half filled with candy and gum wrappers, aluminum cans and soda bottles as Chelsea walked the nature trail, searching for litter. Well, that was the excuse she'd given the manager of the nature center for staying on after the center had closed.

Actually, she'd come here after-hours, with the gate locked tight against visitors, because she knew it was the one place she could be utterly alone.

She'd spent more than an hour wandering the trails, picking up bits of paper and glass that were inevitably left behind by the public. No amount of pleading or preaching would stop some people from polluting the landscape.

A plastic straw lay at the base of a tall oak tree and Chelsea bent to pick it up. She stuffed it into the bag, then simply stood there listening to the quiet.

She desperately wished her thoughts were as serene as these woods. Reflections of everything May had said about marriage had been whirling around in her brain. If her mind was a slate, she could simply wipe it clean and rid herself of all these tormenting ideas.

Loving Ben, wanting him, longing to be a real wife to him, needing—craving—to touch his soul. But it was futile, when she couldn't give one hundred percent of herself. She couldn't trust.

But even if she could, the whole idea of loving Ben was a futile one, because he didn't feel the same. How could she ever begin to imagine that Ben might feel something for her? How could he love someone like her? Someone who hadn't even been loved by her own mother? It was silly. No, it was stupid.

She *knew* she was unlovable. She'd known it for years and years now. She'd even come to accept the idea. And then Ben came along.

Kind, caring, generous Ben.

Just the thought of him was enough to put a smile on her face.

Abruptly, she cocked her head and looked back along the trail behind her. She'd thought she'd heard something. There it was again.

Dropping the plastic garbage bag, she took several steps back the way she had come.

Then she heard it. Faintly but clearly, Chelsea heard the sound of someone calling her name. She went toward the sound and realized it was Ben.

"Over here," she called.

The winding trail was flanked by thick underbrush and tall trees, and it was several minutes and several back-and-forth calls before he came into view.

"I've been calling forever," he said. "I was just about to give up and go home."

"There are miles and miles of trails," Chelsea told him. "It's a wonder we found one another."

"It sure is. May told me I could find you here."

"Is everything okay?" she asked.

"Everything's fine," he said. "I just thought we'd spend some time together."

"Oh." After a moment, she asked, "How did you get in? The gate to the parking lot is locked."

Ben grinned. "I parked on the entrance road and jumped over the gate. Pretty spry for an old guy, huh?"

She chuckled softly, her heart melting at the sight of his boyish smile. "Yeah, pretty spry." Then she added, "I have to go back." She indicated the trail behind her. "I've been picking up litter and I left the bag when I heard you calling."

"That's okay," he said. "I'll come, too. I wanted to get you out alone in the woods, anyway."

She laughed out loud when she saw his eyebrows waggle mischievously.

"What do you mean?" And for the first time, she realized that she'd been so intent on looking at his handsome face that she hadn't noticed the thick, fluffy quilt that he had slung over his forearm.

"Well," he began, his tone light, "I thought we'd go deep into this desolate, isolated forest and...talk."

Again she laughed, knowing very well he was teasing. He certainly didn't mean for them to...to... But surely he didn't want to... In the woods?

No, there was no double meaning in his words. He simply wanted to talk. And rib her a little.

They walked the trail and when they came to the plastic bag that she'd dropped, she bent to retrieve it.

"Let it be," Ben said. "We'll get it on the way back."

"Okay. But how far do you want to go?"

"Oh, just far enough," he said, the words still tinged with teasing. "I'll let you know."

They rounded a sharp bend in the trail and came upon a tiny clearing.

"This looks good," he said. He reached down and tossed aside a small branch from the grassy spot. The blanket covered the entire area as if it were made to fit.

Ben eased himself onto the quilt and patted a spot beside him. "Have a seat," he offered.

Sitting down cross-legged, she asked, "So, what'd you want to discuss?"

"Money."

"Oh?" She couldn't hide her surprise. She hadn't known what to expect, but she wouldn't have guessed this topic in a million years.

"Yes," he said. "I'm a little concerned about the business, and I thought I'd ask your opinion."

Her astonishment must have been evident, because his sigh held a touch of impatience.

"Chels," he said, "you *are* the bookkeeper. You work with the numbers everyday."

"Of course," she said, finally understanding. She felt a bit chagrined at having thought he wanted her opinion simply because it was *her* opinion. But, of course, thinking that for even a split second had been silly of her. He wanted her counsel because she was his employee—his bookkeeper.

"Well," she said, "the numbers have been tight lately. But we're still operating in the black."

"Barely." He nearly growled the word.

"Now, it's not as bad as all that. I've seen it worse while John Reed was in charge."

"You did?" he asked

"Um-hmm," she answered. "The profit you're looking at now is just slightly below average for all the years I worked for your grandfather."

He ran his fingers through his hair, an action Chelsea had become so conscious of this past week. It always started a giddiness churning in her stomach.

"Chels, I want the business to prosper," he said. "I want Reed's Orchard to grow and succeed past my grandfather's dreams."

"But," she started slowly, not wanting to hurt him, "John Reed is gone, Ben. Why are you—"

"Past *my* dreams, then," he said in a rush. "I know he's gone, but I want him to—" he hesitated "—if he could be here now, or look down and see me...I want him to be proud."

"I'm sure he would be," she said softly. "You saved the orchard from being sold, didn't you?"

"You did that," he said. Then his frustration boiled over. "Is it too much to ask to be a success?"

"Of course not."

"Well, how can I achieve what I'm looking for?"

She tipped her head slightly. "You *are* talking money, aren't you? You want more personal wealth from the orchard."

He sighed, as though he was weighing his answer. "I'm not looking to become a millionaire. But more money would be nice. I guess I'd like a little recognition."

"I'm not following you."

He pressed his strong hands together and touched his index fingers to his lips. She looked at those hands and those lips and experienced a nearly tangible flashback of the pleasure they gave her in bed.

Chelsea's mouth nearly dropped open at the vivid image. She swallowed back the gasp that welled in her throat.

"I want the people in the surrounding community to know we're here," he said. "I want them to know what it is we do. I want them to respect the work...the effort we put into making Reed's Orchard—'' He broke off suddenly, then shook his head in frustration. "I don't know what I want."

She took a deep breath and collected herself, tried to focus on the conversation at hand.

After running her tongue over her lips, she said, "I think I understand. And I think that in order to command respect for your hard work, you have to let people see what it is that you do."

His brow rose with interest at her words.

"Open up the orchard to the public," she offered. "I don't know...maybe offer hayrides in the evenings...or..." Then she got excited as an idea fell into her head. "How about offering local elementary schools a tour. Let the children see what it's like to run a fruit-growing business."

"That's a great idea," he said. "Kids would love seeing the refrigeration room where we store the apples."

"And the sorting machine, and the bagging machine, and the conveyor belts. Children probably have no idea where those apples at the supermarket come from. You'll be enlightening the worlds of lots of children...." She lifted one shoulder. "And the school system will be enlarging our profit margin."

"Chels, this is a wonderful idea." His gem green eyes glowed with excitement. "Wonderful. Thanks."

A delicious warmth permeated Chelsea's whole being. She'd made Ben happy. She'd never before made another person smile as he was smiling right now. It felt good. No, it felt great.

He reached out and took hold of her fingers. "I want to change the topic now," he said.

His gaze turned dark and somber.

"I want you to know how sorry I am that you were so disappointed about . . . not being pregnant."

She nodded and looked down at the quilt. "It was a combination of frustration and hormones. I really made too much out of it. I shouldn't have acted so—"

"No," he said, lifting her chin with his crooked fingers.

Their gazed met and locked.

"I understand how badly you want a baby," he said. "And I understand why."

Chelsea felt he could never fully comprehend her reasons behind wanting a child, but she remained silent. It was enough that he tried. More than enough. His concern for her made her chest ache with love for him.

He reached up and touched her cheek. "I know it's been a good week since—" here his sentence trailed off for a moment "—well, since your disappointment . . . and I was wondering if . . . if . . ." Again his voice faded.

She knew what he was trying to say and she smiled at his delicate attempt to ask if her monthly cycle was complete.

Blinking slowly, she nodded. "Everything's fine," she told him. "We can try again."

"Good," he said, his mouth drawing into a charming grin. "Because I've been looking forward to trying again."

He moved closer, his fingers sliding to the pulse point of her neck. Her surprise and alarm forced her heart to quicken.

"But, Ben, you can't mean...you really don't want to...here?"

His smile widened and his eyes took on an almost mesmerizing glint. "You're having trouble saying the words again," he murmured. "I want to make love to you here in the woods. Is there some reason we shouldn't?"

The question was sultry and sensuous, and Chelsea's tongue flicked out nervously to lick at her dry lips.

"But I've never...I don't think I could..."

He chuckled, a deep, rich sound emanating from the back of his throat. A tingling excitement gathered inside her.

"I've never made love outside, either," he said, his timbre seductively enticing. "But haven't you ever imagined what it would be like?"

All the while he'd been moving closer and closer, and Chelsea was shocked to realize that he was only a scant millimeter from her. She felt like the overpowered prey of a hypnotizing cobra—the overpowered, yet willing prey. She looked into his enthralling eyes and melted against him. It took very little effort for him to ease her back onto the quilt.

"No," she whispered, swallowing around the sudden constriction in her throat. "I've never imagined."

He rubbed his chin along her jawline. "You know what I'd like?" he asked.

"What would you like?" Her response was hushed and automatic, as though she had no control over her own voice.

"I would like, years from now, for you to look back on this time you've spent conceiving your child as happy—" He unfastened the top button of her blouse. "Exciting—" He unfastened the next button. "And adventurous." He unfastened yet another button and slipped his hand inside. His warm fingers glided across her lower rib cage and Chelsea inhaled sharply.

She closed her eyes when she felt his moist lips touch her chin. And when he took her bottom lip between his teeth she tilted her face and kissed him.

He smelled so wonderful, felt so good. She was comfortable with her role in their lovemaking by this time and didn't hesitate to part her lips as an offer for him to deepen the kiss. The fact that he accepted the offer elated her.

Ben pulled away and she raised her eyelids. His green gaze was dark with passion. It saddened her just a bit to realize that his desire was purely physical, but right now that didn't seem to matter at all.

Leaning on one elbow, he guided her arms above her head and then unfastened the remaining buttons of her blouse, his fingers playing lightly over her stomach as he pushed the material aside. The nerves just under the surface of her skin tingled at his touch and her breath quickened.

"You're beautiful," he whispered.

His tone was husky, and Chelsea closed her eyes and reveled in how his compliment made her feel. She knew very well he didn't mean the words he said—that he was only playing a game. A game he took very seriously.

His object in this game was to make her pregnant, and in order to do that he had to stoke the fires of his desire.

The way he touched her and the things he said were only a part of that game. But she'd decided weeks ago to become a willing participant. The fact that she enjoyed it so much was simply an unexpected extra—one she planned to savor to the fullest extent.

A sigh escaped her lips when she felt his warm, moist mouth press a kiss on the hollow of her throat. His lips moved lower as he planted tiny kisses along the swell of her breast. The heat of his breath brushing across her flesh tantalized and delighted her.

The passion he kindled in her picked up her self-consciousness about being out in the open with him like this and whisked it away to some far-off place.

If he wanted to make love to her here in the woods, then she would let him. If he wanted her to romp naked among the trees, she would. If the truth be known, at this moment she would do anything he asked. Anything.

Chapter Eight

Chelsea paced her small bedroom—back and forth, back and forth—and then sat down on the edge of the firm mattress again. She'd paced and sat at least a dozen times during what seemed the longest three minutes of her life.

She'd left the home pregnancy test on the bathroom shelf while the chemicals worked to determine whether or not she was going to have a baby. Her bedroom had been the most logical place for her to wait, otherwise she knew she wouldn't have been able to take her eyes off the small white plastic contraption that could confirm or deny her hopes and dreams.

When the digital clock on her bedside table flipped from 8:07 to 8:08, Chelsea took a deep breath, stood and methodically made her way to the bathroom.

The blue applicator tip told her all she needed to know. She was pregnant.

The emotions that converged on her were kaleidoscopic: euphoria, joy, satisfaction, fascination, and these she could identify and understand. She'd expected to feel these things, had even looked forward to feeling them. But she became confused when, along with the good emotions, shadows of apprehension, fear and near panic swept through her all at the same time.

Her hands inadvertently closed over her lower abdomen and she looked down. Her mouth suddenly became dry as sand, as feelings of dread and concern crowded her mind.

This baby was everything she wanted. She had sacrificed so much to conceive this beloved child. She had even opened herself to Ben in a way that she'd promised herself she never would, all for the sake of having this baby.

But what kind of mother would she make? she wondered. Would she be able to give this baby all it would need in life? Would she be able to make it on her own?

She glanced into the mirror, her stark, pale face revealing the truth. The last question that passed through her mind was the one that really concerned her. And to be one hundred percent honest with herself, she had to admit that the real question was: Would she be able to make it without Ben?

The love she felt for him nearly burst her heart at times. Life without him would be bleak and desolate. Life without him—

She shoved the thought from her. She'd made a deal with Ben. She had promised that once she'd become pregnant, she would leave Reed's Orchard.

Ben didn't love her. She knew that. Ben would never love her. She knew that, too.

Glancing down, she concentrated on where her palms pressed against her lower stomach. Ben would never love her, but she'd have a small piece of him—a piece of him that she would love and cherish forever.

Thoughts of the baby growing inside her intensified her emotions until the pure happiness she felt veiled all her doubts and fears.

She could give her child all the love and care that she'd never received. A huge smile took over her whole face. Yes, her dream was finally coming true. She was going to have a baby.

The early June morning was chilly and Chelsea tugged on a sweater before she started through the orchard on her way to work. The gray overcast sky did nothing to diminish the lighthearted gaiety that quickened her step.

She couldn't wait to tell Ben about the baby.

That thought made her step falter and she stopped. Her successful conception meant that there would be no more nights spent in Ben's passionate embrace—no more kisses that turned her blood hot with molten desire.

Crossing her arms over her chest, she contemplatively rubbed her hands up and down her upper arms. Her heart felt as tender and vulnerable as the tiny, newly forming fruit on the trees around her.

She tilted her chin with determination. She'd known the course her marriage would take from the beginning of her deal with Ben. She had known this time would come.

Granted, she'd never thought she would fall in love with Ben. But her feelings for him didn't change the terms of their agreement.

She would tell him right away, this morning if she could find him. And then they could work out the best time for her to gather her things and leave Reed's Orchard.

Rounding the building, Chelsea pushed her way through the door as she'd done a million times before. Her emotions were churning with such a strong mixture of bliss and sadness that she was afraid the turmoil would prove too much for her.

As she passed the side entrance to the store she heard May's voice.

"Chelsea?" May called.

Chelsea turned and went into the shop.

"Good morning, May," she said, hearing the shakiness of her voice.

"What's wrong?" May asked.

"Wrong?" She shook her head. "Nothing's wrong. I'm..." Hesitating only the barest moment, she smiled. "I'm pregnant."

"Why, Chelsea, that's wonderful." May threw her arms around Chelsea. But after a quick hug she pulled back, her face suddenly crestfallen. "But that means you'll be leaving us soon."

A knot formed in Chelsea's throat and she only nodded.

"But I was only just getting to know you," May said. "Maybe you could stay on a while. Just until the baby's born? I'd love to see the little tyke. And I know Ben would, too."

When Chelsea shook her head, she knew the action was more terse than she'd meant for it to be. But it was hard to manage her outward body language and fight for control of her inner emotions at the same time.

"I'm afraid not," she said. "It wouldn't be a good idea."

"But you and Ben have gotten along so well. Maybe—"

"No, May." Her tone was emphatic now. "I can't stay. A clean break would be best."

Her heart broke when she saw the hurt look that crossed May's plump face. Her words hadn't been meant to injure May, only to create some distance between them.

Purposefully withdrawing from this woman whom she'd come to love made Chelsea feel lousy, but it was time for her to leave Reed's Orchard behind. She had to protect herself from as much hurt as she possibly could. Retreating emotionally now was the best thing for both of them. She had to look away from May's dispirited gaze.

"Does Ben know?"

Shaking her head negatively, Chelsea said, "He left the house early, to get as much outside work completed as possible. The weather report called for rain. Do you know where I can find him? I'd like to tell him."

"I'm not sure where he is," May said. "I've been trying to raise him on the two-way radio. I heard reports of hail."

"Hail."

The word sent fear racing through her. Hail was a nightmare for fruit growers. Hailstorms and the wind that came with them could wreak irreparable damage on the delicate fruit crop. An abrupt hailstorm could also spell danger to the workers who had the misfortune to be caught in one.

"Ben should know," Chelsea said, her voice raising a little with sudden tension. "You couldn't reach him on the radio?"

"No. There was nothing but static."

"I'll go look for him."

"But Chelsea," May said, "it isn't safe for you to be driving around. The sky is getting darker every second. Even if the weather doesn't bring hail, it looks as if it will at least pour cats and dogs."

That was when the first rumblings of thunder shattered the silence of the sky.

"I've got to go, May," Chelsea said. "I have to let Ben know about the hail report. The men could be hurt if they don't know to take shelter."

She hurried to the door. "You keep trying to reach him by radio."

"I will," May assured her. "You be careful."

Chelsea ran to Ben's office and grabbed the keys to one of the orchard pickup trucks. She burst through the door and out into the parking lot.

The sky was ominously dark, the thunderclouds gathering with terrifying speed. The wind was strengthening, whipping at her hair as she made her way to the pickup. The engine turned over and Chelsea pulled onto the narrow country road.

A bolt of lightning flashed across the sky and Chelsea jumped. The growing fear that Ben might be caught out in this precarious weather made it hard for her to decide where to go in search of him. She decided to try to get in front of the storm.

Driving a little faster than was safe, Chelsea scanned the land for some sight of Ben and the men.

Damn it! If she hadn't come to love Ben, her heart wouldn't be racing in her chest right now, panic wouldn't be clogging her throat and making it hard for her to breathe. Where was he?

She searched two more groves of trees before she saw several dark green trucks just like the one she was driving. Pulling onto the dirt track that led through the orchard, she felt a tremendous relief when she saw a group of men coming over the ridge.

The rear end of the truck skidded a bit as she came to a stop. She opened the door and glanced over her shoulder to see the storm was quickly approaching.

"Where's Ben?" she called to the men.

They gestured behind them and continued on their way to the parked trucks.

"I'm here, Chels," Ben said. "What are you doing out in this weather?"

"I've been looking for you." She was surprised by the breathlessness of her voice. "I wanted to tell you about the storm."

His mouth split into a grin as he remarked, "You don't think I have enough sense to get in out of the rain?"

She wanted so badly to throw her arms around him, kiss him and tell him she was happy he was safe. But she didn't.

"May heard reports of hail," she told him.

He shouted orders at the men, then reached into his pocket and tossed his keys to one of them. The men got into the vehicles and drove away. Ben took Chelsea by the arm and started toward her truck.

"You shouldn't have come out."

She was jolted by the angry tone of his voice.

"But May couldn't reach you on the radio," she tried to explain.

Without thought, his free hand went to the receiver that was hooked to his belt.

"There was so much static," he said. "I thought the weather must be causing it, so I turned it down. It was stupid of me."

They got into the cab of the truck and Ben started the engine.

"But you still shouldn't have come out," he said. "You could have had an accident on the wet roads. Anything could have happened."

"But—"

"I'll take you back to the office. And I want you to stay there."

"You won't be staying?" she asked.

"I can't, Chels." His eyes were glued to the road ahead of them. "I have to go see what's going on."

"Then, let me go with you," Chelsea pleaded.

"No. It's best if you stay inside," he said.

"I want to go," she said. "I want to be there for you if..." She let her voice fade, unwilling to speak the possibilities.

He didn't answer, he simply drove on in silence. Chelsea didn't know if he was planning on taking her back to the office or not.

When he reached the intersection and didn't turn toward the office, she knew she'd be going with him. Again she was flooded with a sense of relief that astounded her.

Ben drove toward the storm front, and the first gust of wind that hit the truck made Chelsea gasp. She clutched her hands together in her lap and watched the sky darken as they drove into the dense curtain of rain.

The silence was a heavy shroud in the cab of the pickup. Ben concentrated on driving in the blinding torrent; Chelsea fought back her fear of what damage the weather might inflict on the orchard.

Chelsea turned her gaze on Ben and she saw him lean forward just enough to pull the radio receiver free from its holder on his belt.

"May, this is Ben," he said after pushing the transmitter button. "Are you there?"

He repeated the call and May's voice sounded faint in the midst of the static.

"I'm here, Ben," May said.

"Did the men get back safely?"

"Everyone came in and I sent them on home for the rest of the morning," she said. "Is Chelsea with you?"

"She's here," Ben said.

"You two should—"

May's voice broke up in the loud crackling.

"We'll be in soon," Ben said, raising his voice in the hopes that his aunt would hear.

"Hail southeast of town—"

The rest of what May had said was drowned in a sea of static.

After hearing May's report, Ben and Chelsea looked at one another.

"The peaches."

Ben's tone was strained, and the anxiety in the pit of Chelsea's stomach churned sickeningly.

He switched off the receiver and immediately turned the truck in a southeasterly direction.

In less than ten minutes he was turning onto the dirt track that led back to the peach orchard. Hail had begun to strike the roof of the truck with tiny pings.

Chelsea hadn't realized she'd been holding her breath until her cerebral impulses forced her to suck in air. She exhaled and felt a shiver shimmy up her spine.

"How bad is it?" She couldn't help but ask Ben, even though she knew very well that the two of them were looking out the same windshield, seeing the same slight incline that hid the orchard from view.

Ben shifted into a lower gear. And as the truck slowly climbed the hill, Chelsea could tell the hailstones were growing larger. It was as though rocks were being thrown at the roof and windshield of the truck.

"Oh, Lord," Ben murmured as he pushed his foot against the brake pedal and brought the truck to a stop.

The wind whipped the trees as the hail pummeled the young fruit relentlessly, viciously. Broken branches flew across their view like tumbleweed.

Ben and Chelsea could only sit there and helplessly watch the stones of ice destroy the peach crop.

The weather worsened. The sound of the hail hitting the cab became deafening. One stone the size of a large nut crashed down on the truck, denting its hood.

"Let's get out of here," Ben said, his voice hoarse with stress.

He executed a three-point turn and steered the truck back toward the paved road.

Chelsea felt trapped by the silence that lay between them. She knew he was hurting, she knew he was worried sick, but she didn't know how to make things better. She couldn't seem to find the words that would make this bleak situation any brighter.

A thought flashed through her mind: her baby. Automatically, her hand went to her stomach. A part of the man she loved was inside her, growing, developing with every passing moment. The very idea brought her a tremendous peace—a peace she only wished she could share with Ben.

But she couldn't possibly tell him about her pregnancy now. He certainly didn't feel the way she did about the baby. No, she couldn't burden him with her good news when he was experiencing such a crisis.

Ben switched off the engine and simply sat there. The rain had subsided to a steady pattering and the wind tapered off to intermittent gusts.

"I'm sorry," Chelsea finally said.

Although her apology would do him no good, she was awed by the amount of emotion her words held. This man had succeeded in stirring her feelings as no one had in many years.

Ben rested his elbow on the curve of the steering wheel, his chin cupped in his palm.

"I wanted to succeed," he said.

"But Ben," she said. "You're helpless against the weather."

He didn't seem to hear. Or maybe he did, and he chose to ignore the simple truth.

"We needed the rain," he commented. "But the hail..." He rubbed his forehead with his fingertips. "The hail was a killer."

Chelsea turned and rested her back against the passenger door so she was facing him.

"It's too bad there's no insurance." It wasn't a question. She paid the bills and knew she'd never written a single check to cover an insurance premium.

"Insurance would erode the profits too deeply," Ben said. "I insure the buildings and equipment, and that's all I can afford. If I secured the crops, I'd never be able to improve the business. New equipment or acreage."

He chuckled ironically. "Granddad felt that farmers are gamblers by nature. I always knew what he meant. But now that he's not here to chuck me softly on the chin and assure me that everything's going to be all right, I not only know what he meant, I feel it. Hell, I'm living it. And it isn't very pleasant.''

"Well, maybe it's not as bad as it looked."

He made a disgusted sound. "Come on, Chels. You saw the same thing I did.''

She gazed out the windshield at the apple trees that lined the land in back of the house. She had seen the devastation; she knew it was most probably worse than what it had looked. There were acres and acres of peach trees in that particular grove. The hailstorm had most likely destroyed every bit of the peach crop.

Although it wasn't like her, she couldn't bring herself to be negative.

"But you really won't know for sure," she said, "until you go and check it out."

"And I will," he answered. "Later."

He reached over and covered her hand with his.

"I want to thank you for going with me. It meant a lot.''

They sat there, motionless, his hand on hers. He searched her face and then turned his gaze to the scenery beyond the window.

Chelsea focused on his face; his deep green eyes, which portrayed such anguish; his strong jaw, which was set and stiff, his mouth taut with the dismay that obviously plagued his mind. She wished she could ease his apprehension, wished she could alleviate his trouble.

The love she felt for him welled inside her until she was frightened her feelings might spill over. His fingers curled around into her palm and she held them tightly. He made a tiny arc on the back of her hand with his thumb.

Closing her eyes, she pressed her free hand over the spot where their baby snuggled and thought about the three of them here together. Even in the midst of this catastrophe, she felt happiness. With Ben holding her hand and her baby cuddled inside her, she somehow felt they were, for that moment, connected. She might never have another chance to feel this way.

If only Ben could find the same kind of comfort she was experiencing.

They stayed at home the rest of that rainy day. Ben paced from room to room like a restless, silent phantom. Chelsea couldn't get him to eat any of the lunch or the dinner she'd prepared. She ended up eating both meals alone, if picking at the food and moving it from place to place on her plate could be called eating.

She washed up the dishes by hand, rather than using the electric dishwasher. And just to keep busy, she spent an unnecessarily long time straightening the cabinets that held the pots and pans, baking dishes and cookie sheets.

Finally, with absolutely nothing left to clean or organize, she went into the living room, drying her hands on a tea towel as she went.

Ben sat in the evening gloom on the far corner of the sofa. When she reached to turn on the lamp, he said, "Don't. Please."

She sat down beside him. "Ben, you'll make it through this."

In the shadows, she saw him nod.

"I know I will," he said, his voice thick with emotion. "I've just been thinking of the men."

"The men who work for you?" she asked.

"Yes. I'm sure the loss of the peach crop will force me to lay some of them off." He sighed heavily.

He was silent as he rubbed an agitated hand over his jaw. "Those men have families to feed, bills to pay."

Chelsea looked down and saw that she'd twisted the linen towel into a tight snake. Why couldn't she lift some of this heavy weight from his shoulders?

He stood suddenly and looked down at her. "At times like this, it isn't fun to be the business owner. It isn't fun, at all."

Ben pulled open the door and walked out.

Chelsea went to the window and watched him tramp off through the orchard.

She had to do something. She simply had to find some way to help him out of this mess.

The loss wasn't enough to make Reed's Orchard go under, but she could see that Ben was eating himself inside out worrying about his employees—men who needed the jobs he provided.

Her mind churned with possibilities. And as it did, she absently twisted the towel ever tighter.

Chapter Nine

Chelsea knocked on the door of Ben's office twice, excitement over her idea compelling her to rush inside before he could answer.

"You left before I got up this morning," she said brightly.

The sight of his haggard face wrenched at her heart and caused her smile to fade. It was obvious that he hadn't slept. The white pad of paper that lay on the desk in front of him had a long, neat line of numbers written on it. He punched the buttons of a calculator without looking up.

"I left at dawn to check out the peach crop," he said. "It's completely wiped out. Completely."

"I'm sorry, Ben."

He dropped the pencil on top of the pad and gazed at her. "I've been trying to work out some numbers—" he sighed heavily "—but I guess I should have waited for you."

"I'll be happy to help you with the figures," she told him. Then a spontaneous smile pulled at her mouth as she said, "But I think I can help you even more than simply working out some numbers."

His brow furrowed as he asked, "What are you talking about?"

"Well," she began. She shrugged. "This should explain everything."

She handed him the slip of paper. He reached out and took it, his brow still displaying his perplexity.

"It's a check," he said.

"Um-hmm."

"A personal check," he said.

"Um-hmm."

He leveled his bewildered green eyes on her.

"For fifty thousand dollars." His husky voice sounded more than a little bewildered.

"Um-hmm."

Leaning back in his chair, he rubbed the knuckle of his index finger across his lips. He sat there in silence studying her.

She eased herself down in the chair facing him and gave him the time he needed to collect his thoughts.

It was a perfect idea. One that had come to her in the wee hours of the morning. She had scrimped and saved for nearly ten years and that money was sitting in her bank account just waiting for the chance to help Ben.

Well, the money hadn't really been meant to help Ben, and giving it to him would mean that she wouldn't be able to leave Reed's Orchard as soon as she'd planned. But she could live with that. She'd simply have to work hard and continue to scrimp and save. But that shouldn't be too difficult—it had become a way of life.

A tiny voice had whispered in her mind that giving Ben her money was a good excuse for staying. But she'd stifled the whispers—cut them off at the quick— and convinced herself that providing an excuse for staying wasn't the reason she was offering Ben her savings.

Her sole objective was to help Ben out of this terrible predicament. And from the look on his face, he was totally amazed by her suggestion.

His tone was somber and quiet when he said, "This is the money you've saved. The money you planned to use to get settled somewhere else."

"Um-hmm," she confirmed, but the look on his face and the tone of his voice dimmed her excitement and optimism, and the pitch of her answer wasn't as bright as before.

"Why would you give me your money?"

His question caught her off guard. She hadn't expected him to ask what had motivated her to give him the money. And she certainly couldn't ever tell him the truth.

"What do you mean 'why'?" she asked, playing for time. "Do I need a reason?"

"Yes, you do," he said. "I want to know why you'd give me something so important to you, something that took you years to save. I mean, leaving here after you become pregnant *is* important to you isn't it?"

"Of course it is." Her tone was almost haughty.

"Then why would you do this?"

Her tongue darted out to moisten her suddenly dry lips. "Well," she began. She stopped long enough to swallow. "I know that my money will cover only a small fraction of the loss. But if you accept it, you won't have to lay off the men."

He started to speak, but she charged ahead. "Not right away, anyway. That money will keep those men employed for a few months more. Those men have families. They have bills to pay. They need their jobs. You said as much last night." She knew she was rambling, but she couldn't help it. "I'll continue to save and—" she shrugged one shoulder "—who knows, maybe the fall harvest will bring enough profit so that you'll be able to repay me."

Her rush of words was a diversion, a smokescreen she hoped would distract him from his original question.

Ben leaned forward and rested one elbow on his desk top. "But what if you become pregnant before the fall harvest? What if you want to leave before then? And what if the profits aren't enough to enable me to pay you back right away?"

In her agitation, she stood and rounded the chair, fighting the urge to run away from his questions. She should have told him about the baby last night. Now, he'd never accept her help. How could she explain why she was offering her life savings to him, when she had successfully conceived a child and it was time for her to leave Reed's Orchard? She couldn't even explain it to herself. She faced him, her hands gripping the chair back.

"Ben, I don't have all the answers. I was only trying to—"

Chelsea was interrupted by May pushing open the door of Ben's office.

"Good morning, you two," May said, then she directed her attention to Ben. "I'm sorry about the peach crop. Have you checked out just how bad it is?"

"Totally destroyed," Ben told her. "I'd be surprised if the harvest equalled even a few bushel baskets."

"That bad?" May asked.

Ben only nodded.

"We'll survive this," May said. "We've survived worse."

"I hope you're right."

May placed her hand on Chelsea's shoulder, but continued to address Ben. "What do you think of Chelsea's news?"

Chelsea felt her insides freeze.

"We were just talking about it," Ben said. "I think it would be wrong for me to take her money."

Realizing that he was confusing issues, Chelsea tried to break into the conversation by speaking Ben's name, but neither Ben nor May responded. Other than being outright rude, Chelsea could see no other recourse but to stand there and helplessly listen to May delivering news that *she* should have imparted yesterday.

"Money?" May asked. "I don't know what money you're talking about, but I'm talking about the baby."

Bewilderment passed fleetingly across Ben's face before his gaze sought out and locked on Chelsea's. She wanted so badly to look away, but his expression refused to release her.

"I didn't get a chance to tell you," she said weakly.

"You didn't know?" May asked, her tone horrified. "I'm sorry, Ben. It's obvious you two need to talk. I'll come back later."

The door closed, leaving Ben and Chelsea alone with the awkward silence that lay between them. Neither one spoke, they only stared at one another. Chelsea tried hard to sense what he might be feeling. Was he angry that she hadn't told him? Was he—?

"When did you find out?" His question was spoken in a hushed, tenebrous, almost angry tone.

Chelsea swallowed with difficulty. "Yesterday morning. I meant to let you know immediately. But then May told me about the hail, and I went to find you." She looked down at her hands and then back to him. "I actually forgot for a while. But then when the baby came to my mind again, you were feeling so bad that I . . . I didn't think it was a good time to give you the news."

He inhaled deeply, his slight nod told her he understood her reasons for failing to tell him right away.

His gaze never wavered as he said, "You'll be leaving now."

The finality in the sound of his words crushed her. It was so decisive, so terminal.

"But, Ben, I don't have to leave right away," she tried. "You'll need a bookkeeper. I'm willing to stay long enough to train whoever you hire."

"Chelsea." Her name exploded from him in a burst. "You'll be staying much longer than that."

His eyes narrowed with anger or frustration, Chelsea couldn't tell which. But at the sight of them, her stomach tightened with trepidation.

"Did you forget that you've given me the money that was supposed to get you away from here?"

He stood up now, his shoulders tense, his back straight.

"Here." He thrust her check at her, his barely controlled outrage making his hand shake. "Take this. I can't allow you to give me money that you'll need."

Reaching out, she gently plucked the check from his grasp with trembling fingers.

His reaction confused her. Why was he so angry?

Then it came to her, and she understood perfectly. In proposing that he use her money, she had offered him a solution to his problem, but then she'd jerked it away. That's why he was angry.

She wanted so badly to help him, but the only way to do that now would be to *force* him to take her check. But if she did that, he'd realize the truth—that helping him meant more to her than fulfilling her plans of leaving. Her mind whirled with another truth—*he* meant more to her than the hopes and dreams she'd nurtured for years.

Feeling as if she were moving in slow motion, she folded the check and slipped it into her pocket. She could never let him know her feelings. She'd never survive being rejected by him.

"I'm still willing to stay long enough to train someone to do my job," she said quietly. "In fact, I'll...I'll look for someone. I'll call the paper and place an advertisement in the employment section."

He searched her eyes for a moment before answering, "I'd appreciate that."

They stood in the thick silence; she, feeling disheartened and guilty that she was unable to help Ben, and he, looking tormented by the problem that weighed heavily on him.

"Well, I should go," she said. "I have plenty of work to do."

She was at the door when he called her name and she turned back to face him.

"Don't wait dinner for me," he said. "I'll be late clearing up the peach grove."

Her hand automatically went to her tummy. "Now that I've conceived, there's really no reason for me to stay at your house. I'll move my things out today."

It killed her to say the words. But she had to make a clean break now, or she might never find the strength.

Ben watched his office door close behind Chelsea and felt his whole world was falling apart. He'd never felt so alone in his life.

A knock at the door sent his hopes soaring.

"Chels?"

"No," May said, opening the door and coming inside. "It's only me. I came to share this outlandish news article with you. Do you believe that these scientists have taken pictures of a covered wagon that they found on the moon?"

"Aunt May, you really shouldn't believe—"

"Everything I read," May finished for him. "I know, I know."

Ben closed his eyes a moment, and then looked at his aunt. "I'm really not in the mood to hear any of your tabloid stories."

"Okay, okay," May said.

"I'm sorry, Aunt May," Ben said. "It's just that I'm in an awful mess."

"I know. It's awful what Old Man Weather did to us."

Ben shook his head. "I'm not talking about that," he said. "Chelsea's leaving."

May gazed at him a moment before replying, "I thought that was the plan."

He nodded. "It was. I was certain that, to save my orchard, I could marry Chelsea, make her pregnant and let her go."

Reaching up, he massaged a sudden ache at the back of his neck. His voice was pensive as he said, "But it appears that I've fallen in love with my wife."

May eased herself down in her chair to listen, and Ben followed suit. He looked at his aunt across his desk, knowing full well that his eyes held a haunted look.

"When I first married Chels, she was so stiff, so solemn. I started a campaign to see how often I could make her smile. That smile ate its way right into my heart, Aunt May. Like a drug—something I couldn't live without. I began thinking about it all day while I worked. I dreamed about it at night. I lived to see Chelsea's face brighten with that beautiful . . ."

He shook his head. "It sounds so stupid, when I hear the words out loud. But it's true." He lifted one shoulder in a half shrug. "Pretty soon, though, I didn't have to work so hard at making her smile. She began to relax around me. We had such good times when we were together."

Ben rubbed his fingers along his jaw as he contemplated the past couple of months since he'd married Chelsea.

"The very thought of her gave me energy that sustained me through the day. I couldn't wait to get home after work." He chuckled. "I even started letting the men off a little early, so I could get home to Chelsea." After a moment, he remarked, "You know, one day I even went to the nature center looking for her."

Thoughts of the joyous afternoon they'd spent making love in the wild outdoors only seemed to depress him more. No longer would he find in Chelsea a confidante, someone in whom he could confide his doubts about the business as he had confided in his wife that day. No longer would he find in her a lover who surpassed all his imaginings and fulfilled all his silent yearnings.

All the frustration he felt was expressed in a slow, dispirited exhalation.

"Yes, sir," May said. "Sounds like love to me."

He clenched his fist on the desk top. "And now she's leaving."

"So, you told her how you feel and she doesn't feel the same."

"I didn't tell her anything," Ben said.

"Why not?"

That one simple question stumped him for a moment and he sat there with what he was afraid May would describe as a "dumb" look on his face.

"Well," he began, his mind still churning. "I've come to know Chels enough to realize that—" he thought about the misery she'd suffered as a child, how the social workers had lied to her again and again "—actions speak louder to her than words."

He narrowed his eyes at May, as another reason came to mind. "Besides, if I told her how I feel, she simply wouldn't believe me."

May raised her chubby hands into the air. "Well, why in tarnation wouldn't she?" she asked indignantly.

"You see," Ben explained, "Chelsea's mother gave her up when she was just a little girl. Chelsea believes that since her mother didn't love her, then no one else will, either."

"That's plain stupid, if you ask me," May commented, with an unladylike snort.

Ben shook his head. "Somewhere along the line, some asinine social worker put the idea into her head."

"Now, don't degrade every social worker because of one bad apple," May said, shifting her bulk in the chair. "It takes a special kind of person to dedicate his or her life to helping people."

"I understand that," Ben said impatiently. He didn't want to talk about social workers. "But this jerk really messed with Chelsea's head. Along with the fact that her mother gave her up for adoption, and the system took her away from the one lady who wanted her."

He heaved another sigh. "It all adds up to Chelsea feeling that she doesn't deserve to be loved."

"And again I say that's just plain stupid."

"I know it is," Ben replied. "Try telling that to Chelsea."

"No, *you* need to tell her."

Ben felt his frustration boiling over. "I already told you, May. She won't listen to empty words."

"But your words won't be empty," May retorted. "Your words will be full of meaning."

"Chels won't see that," Ben muttered, feeling hopeless and helpless.

"Then *do* something that will show her how you feel," May snapped.

"Like what?"

May gave a disgusted *tsk*. "I feel like I'm back in grade school and there's a pop quiz in math. You cannot peek over at my paper, Ben. I don't know the answer." She rose and went to the door. "You'll have to figure this one out on your own."

"But wait a minute," he said.

"All I *do* know," May said, unheeding of his plea, "is that you have to let Chelsea know how you feel. Whether you tell her or show her, is up to you."

"May!" Ben called.

She turned back one more time, but not in order to listen to him. "Because if you don't," she continued her lecture, "you're going to lose her *and* your baby." Her faded green eyes glared at him. "And I've grown fond of the idea of getting to know my great-great-grandniece or nephew."

Her gaze took on a critical gleam as she said, "I only have one question before I go. If you haven't discussed your feelings with Chelsea, how do you know how she feels? How do you know she really wants to leave?"

"That's two questions." Ben nearly growled the words.

"Oh, my," May said innocently, her wrinkled face splitting with a wide grin. "You would have aced that pop quiz in math, wouldn't you?"

May didn't give him time to think of a rejoinder before she closed the door, and for the second time that morning Ben felt completely and utterly alone.

He picked up the pencil and tapped the eraser on the desk.

Aunt May did have a point. He didn't know how Chelsea felt about him or their marriage.

She cared about him. Or at least she cared about the business. She had shown him that, when she'd offered to give him the money that it had taken her years to accumulate—money that had been meant to settle her and the baby in another part of the country.

But then again, maybe her offer had nothing to do with him. Hadn't she claimed her motivation had been to save the jobs of the men who were employed by him?

Ben leaned back in his chair as a realization struck him. Chelsea had written out the check *after* she'd found out she was pregnant. His brow furrowed deeply as he considered all the implications.

She knew she would be leaving soon, but she'd tried to give him her money anyway. Why?

Did the gesture mean that she really didn't want to leave Reed's Orchard? Or was he reading something between the lines that really wasn't there. He hoped he wasn't.

He accepted the fact that it was hard for her to trust. He even understood why. He had tried so hard to be worthy of her trust. But maybe it wasn't him at all. Maybe she didn't trust *herself* enough to confide in him.

The thought spurred another, more optimistic one; had her actions spoken louder than her words? Could he surmise from Chelsea's offering of her money, that her feelings for him ran deeper than those she chose to reveal?

At the beginning of their relationship, Ben well remembered Chelsea's cold, clinical idea that he was simply a sperm donor who would fertilize her egg, give her a much-wanted child. He knew that her opinion had warmed a little. Hell, there had been times when she had sizzled. He chuckled in spite of his circumstances.

Raking his fingers through his hair, he wondered if he was crazy to think that she might feel something for him.

One thing was certain, he *had* to know Chelsea's true feelings, one way or the other. And he simply had to let her know his.

But how? Telling her was out of the question. He knew very well that she'd never believe mere words. How could he show Chelsea exactly what was in his heart? How could he make her see what she had come to mean to him?

It had to be something big. Something so big that she couldn't mistake his meaning. What could he—?

He sat up straight as an idea struck him with force. Of course! It was perfect.

Deftly, he flipped through the telephone file that sat on his desk and stopped when he found his lawyer's name and number. He punched the buttons on the phone and listened to ringing on the other end of the line.

After speaking to his lawyer's secretary, Ben was put through and he explained what he wanted.

"Can it be done right away, George?" Ben asked, his excitement rising. "I don't care what it costs," Ben responded. "I want it done this week."

What was he saying? This was not a time to be frivolous with money. Not with a loss—

Hell, Chelsea was worth it. What were a few hundred dollars when he was vying for the love of his life?

Ben replaced the receiver, a tiny smile bending one corner of his mouth. He could go into her office right now and tell her what he'd done. But he wanted to wait. He wanted to have the proof in hand when he told her how he felt about her.

He could wait the few days, a week at most, that it would take to get the papers in order. Until then, he'd simply have to hold his tongue and relish the thought of her reaction.

After work, Chelsea let herself into Ben's house for what she knew would be the last time. She'd have to remember to return his key.

She lugged her large suitcase out of the bottom of the closet and began to pack her things. Her chest felt empty and hollow as she folded a pair of jeans and tucked them in the case.

The desolation that filled her became overwhelming. She hated the thought of leaving, but she knew it was inevitable. Keeping up her end of the deal was just as important as keeping her pride.

She'd nearly lost her pride this morning when Ben had cornered her about why she had offered to loan him her money. Luckily, the threatened workers had come to mind and she'd seized the excuse with both hands. She'd blatantly lied in order to avoid telling him she loved him.

Life without him would be a living nightmare. But she'd survive.

Vivid memories of her nights with him called to her from Ben's bedroom and she couldn't help herself—she answered. Tossing aside the cotton camp shirt she'd been folding, she moved with the slow, measured pace of a specter to the doorway of Ben's room.

She stopped short, not daring to cross the threshold. Her bottom lip trembled at the sight of the bed. Here was the spot on which he had taught her what passion was all about. Here was the spot that called to her with irresistible memories—memories of what it was like to make love with the man who meant everything to her.

There would be no more of those nights, as there would be no more picnics, no more walks, no more long talks. He had become more than just her lover, he had become her friend. Now all she had to look forward to were lonely days. And even lonelier nights.

Ben had taught her what love was all about. More than that, he had shown her what it meant to have a true friend. She would miss him.

Hot, salty tears welled in her eyes and slid heedlessly down her face. She pressed her fingers tight against her lips to hold back the sobs that threatened to burst from her. How was she going to survive without Ben?

Closing her eyes, she inhaled deeply, in an effort to get control of her emotions. Emotions she hadn't allowed herself to feel in years. Emotions that Ben had drawn from her. Emotions that he'd reacquainted her with.

Again, the question echoed in her head: How was she going to survive without him?

The calm that settled over her took her by surprise. Her palm moved to cover her lower abdomen at the same moment her baby came to mind.

She would be strong and she would survive, because of the child she carried in her womb. This baby was a little piece of Ben, a piece of him that she'd have forever.

It was good that she was going back to her little brick house for the remainder of her time at the orchard. When she finally left, maybe her craving for Ben would have lessened to a more tolerable level.

Rushing back to her room, she began stuffing items into her suitcase. Shoes on top of dresses, mashed against her alarm clock, shoved next to perfume bottles, hair dryer, brush and comb. There was no rhyme or reason to the packing, just a furious, desperate attempt to escape.

Finally, she was forced to sit on the edge of her bed, breathless and weary. Fresh tears blurred her vision as she finally understood that it didn't matter if she moved a mile away to her tiny ranch house, or two thousand miles away to some unknown city across the country. Nothing would ever lessen the love she felt for Ben. Nothing. And she was doomed to spend the rest of her life yearning for what she could never have.

Chapter Ten

"Chelsea?"

The sound of Ben's voice was like a stabbing pain that made her jerk her head up toward her office door where he stood.

She steeled herself against the emotions simmering inside her, as she had each time she had come into contact with Ben over the past week or so, since she'd told him she was pregnant.

"Yes?"

"Do you have a minute?" he asked. "Can we talk?"

"Sure," she answered, although his questions puzzled her.

Ever since she'd moved from his house, Ben had seemed to go out of his way to avoid her. Their relationship had reverted, digressed even, to what it had been before she'd proposed her deal, before they had married.

It nearly killed her each time she walked past Ben and barely received a smile from him. Knowing and seeing that he'd so easily forgotten what they had shared during their short marriage was like a dull knife that slashed at her heart again and again.

And what was even worse was that horrible little half smile that tugged at his lips every time they met. It was clear evidence of just how relieved he was that his part of the deal had been completed and that she was out of his life for good.

"I have something I want to go over with you," Ben said, moving over to stand in front of her desk.

He'd barely been able to contain himself since he'd contacted his lawyer to have the new deed to the orchard drawn up. So many times he'd nearly told Chelsea what he'd done. He'd had to force himself to turn away, to keep the exciting news from crossing his lips each time he saw her.

But this morning the papers had arrived by courier as he'd requested, and Ben had almost tripped over his own feet in his haste to bring them to Chelsea.

"If it's something concerning the accounts," Chelsea said, "I think you should wait to go over them with the new bookkeeper. I've interviewed one woman who I think will be perfect, but I wanted to get your opinion before I called her to make the final arrangements."

"This has nothing to do with the business," Ben said. "Well, actually it does, but..." His voice faded as he suddenly found himself at a loss for words.

His hesitation obviously conjured confusion in her, and wariness tainted her tone as she asked, "What is it, Ben?"

He'd pictured this scene a thousand times over the past week, each scenario playing out differently in his mind. But he had come to the conclusion that because he wasn't sure of her feelings for him it would be best if he focused his concern *away* from their personal relationship. In order to make her listen and believe what he had to say, he'd have to center his attention on the one thing he was certain they had in common. Their child.

"I know that you're thinking of leaving soon," he said, immediately embarrassed by having stated the blatantly obvious. "I also know...from things you've told me...that you have no family."

He hesitated a moment before continuing, "It bothers me to think that my child might be in need of money or...or..." He threw up his hands. "I don't know much about babies and such, but I want him to have whatever it is he might need."

Her suspicion was now firmly planted in her wrinkled brow, in her narrowed eyes. In a quiet voice, she asked, "Are you saying you don't think I can take care of *my* baby?"

He realized his mistake immediately. She clearly thought of the baby as hers. Not theirs. Not his.

"No," he hurriedly answered, "I'm suggesting no such thing." Trying another tack, he said, "It's just that I've been thinking that I might like to get to know him. I'd like for him to know me."

Her reaction to his words was absolute horror.

"You're going against our original agreement." Her knuckles turned stark white as she tightened her grip on the pen in her hand. "You promised to let me go. You promised me that you wouldn't get involved with—"

"Calm down, Chels," he interrupted.

"Calm down? You've decided to go back on your word and you want me to calm down?"

Hysteria fringed her tone, and the fear in her wide-eyed gaze wrenched his gut.

"I'm only trying to explain…" He shook his head. "I've done something—" he lifted the documents that he held in his hand "— and I'm trying to ease you in to the idea."

"If you feel I need easing in, then you must think I'm not going to like your idea." She was visibly trembling now. "I have to tell you, Ben, so far I don't like anything you've said."

Ben sighed and rubbed the fingers of his free hand across his forehead. He looked at her and took a deep breath, in order that at least one of them could keep a clear head. "This is not going at all as I thought it would." He stepped closer to her, and frowned when she flinched away from him.

"What I've been trying to say is…what I've wanted to tell you…is that I don't want you to leave Reed's Orchard."

He gave her time to respond, and when she didn't he explained further, "I don't want you to go, but whether you go or stay, I want you to know that I've taken care of you and the baby."

She stood. "What are you talking about?"

He'd never heard such hardness in her voice, and it threw him completely off-balance.

"Here," he said, offering her the papers he held in his hand. When she made no move to take them, he lowered his hand to waist level.

He simply couldn't understand her response. Staring down at the deed, his speech took on a mechanical monotone.

"I've put your name on the deed to Reed's Orchard. I've made you half owner. As soon as the baby's born, I'll make him—or her—our sole beneficiary."

There was utter silence on the other side of the desk. Ben had to force himself to lift his gaze to Chelsea's face. Her stony expression nearly knocked the breath from him. He squared his shoulders, determined to finish what he'd started.

"All you have to do is sign at the bottom," he said. "The deed can be recorded and everything will be legal."

Her eyes froze into chips of dark, shiny ice. Her mouth was set firmly, her posture tense.

"I'm not signing anything," she said viciously. "I won't give you any hold on my child."

"What are you talking about?"

"Don't play innocent. I know exactly what you're doing. But you better know that I'll do everything in my power to stop you."

Her chest heaved with suppressed anger.

"I've known from the start how you felt about me," she said. "And you were so certain you would feel the same way about my baby." She lifted her chin. "You were so certain that this baby would mean nothing to you. As I mean nothing. Otherwise, you would never have agreed to our deal."

He watched her throat muscles work as she swallowed with difficulty.

"It's not my fault," she continued, "that your feelings for this child have changed."

Her hand moved to cover her stomach, as if to protect the child inside her.

"It's not my fault," she repeated. "And our original deal still stands. I became your wife so Reed's Orchard wouldn't be sold. I held up my end of the bargain. Now, it's time for you to uphold yours."

"But Chelsea—"

She cut him off with one shaking, upraised hand. "I won't listen to any more. I'm leaving. Today. I'm sorry I wasn't able to train a new bookkeeper." Picking up a manila folder from her desk top, she thrust it toward him. "You'll find the names and telephone numbers of the people I've interviewed in here."

"Wait—"

"No, Ben," she said. "No."

She rounded the desk, her glare a shocking medley of distrust, outrage and pain.

Her pointed finger almost poked his chest as she stated, "Don't look for me. I mean it. I won't let you take my baby, Ben."

The last words she'd uttered paralyzed him. Vaguely, he heard the door slam shut as her declaration rang in his ears.

I won't let you take my baby. I won't let you take my baby.

"What did you do?" May's shrill voice cut through his thoughts as she burst into the office. "What did you say to that child?"

He was helpless to respond.

"What did you say to Chelsea?" May said, her firm tone demanding an answer. "That poor girl ran out of this building sobbing like there was no tomorrow." She plunked a fist on her wide hip. "I want to know what you did."

When he finally found his voice, it sounded as empty as his heart felt. "It backfired, May." He handed her the documents. "I had Chelsea's name put on the deed to the orchard. I wanted to show her how I felt."

"Well," May said, looking over the paperwork, "opening the door on everything you own and inviting her to come in certainly should have showed her your feelings, all right." Her gaze narrowed on him and her voice lowered a notch as she asked, "How did you manage to mess things up?"

"I didn't do anything." The words burst from him. "Somehow she got the crazy notion that I want to take her baby away from her."

"Well, go after her, you idiot! I told you to come right out and tell her how your feel." She rolled her eyes heavenward. "But do you ever listen to me? No. I told you—"

May continued to lecture, but Ben ran out the door.

Chelsea stopped in the middle of the apple orchard to catch her breath. Wiping her eyes on the sleeve of her soft cotton T-shirt, she knew she had to calm herself and think clearly if she was going to get away from here today.

"He wants my baby." She groaned the words aloud and heard their silent, baleful echo through the tree branches.

She felt more alone than she'd ever felt in her entire life. But she really wasn't alone. She laced her fingers over her tummy and cradled her unborn child.

"I'll get us away from here," she promised.

"Chelsea!"

Ben's voice was like an unexpected blast from a trumpet shattering the stillness of the orchard. Her gaze flew to the path behind her and she saw Ben racing toward her.

"Oh, God, please help me." She whispered the tiny prayer and began to run along the path.

But he easily caught up to her and stopped her with a hand on her arm.

"I don't want to talk to you, Ben." She shouted the words at him, struggling to release herself from his grasp.

Tension was evident in every muscle of his body; from the taut lines around his mouth and eyes, to the set of his shoulders. He let go of her, but his clenched fists defined the sinewy muscles of his forearms. A muscle jerked just below the outer corner of his eye and she could see his jaw grind.

"We have to talk." Although his words were quiet, they conveyed ominous emotion.

"I told you—"

"Please, Chels, calm down," Ben said.

"I'm perfectly calm." She knew it was a lie. The anxiety in her stomach was enough to make her dizzy with nausea, but she refused to let him know that.

He reached out to her and she jerked back. He lowered his hand to his side.

"You will listen to what I have to say."

"I will not," she shouted.

"I love you, Chelsea."

Stunned into silence, Chelsea's brow furrowed with confusion. *It's a lie,* her conscience automatically told her. *It's a lie.*

"It's true," he said as if answering the silent chant. "I do love you."

When she finally found her tongue, she snapped, "You really don't expect me to believe that."

The defeated expression that crossed his face surprised her.

"I can't make you believe me," he said. "All I can do is tell you what's in my heart."

She shook her head. "You're doing this because you want the baby." She started to turn away, but it only took the barest touch of his fingertips on her forearm to stop her. She lifted her gaze to his.

"Chels, I understand that you feel you can't give your trust...."

His tone was soft as an apple-blossom petal.

"I can even understand why. Knowing what you went through as a child, it's only natural for you to turn inward, to avoid relationships. Of any kind."

He searched her gaze before continuing, "But I have to tell you...cutting yourself off from everyone around you isn't really living. It's simply existing."

She tried to dip her head away from his, but he caught her chin between his gentle fingers and forced her to look at him.

"Is that what you really want out of life?" he asked.

Chelsea was unable to answer his question, she was unable to speak at all.

"You *do* care about me," he said. "I know that much. You've tried to hide it, but the truth was clear to me when you offered to give me your money." He grimaced. "I may be way off base, but I think you really did it because you care about me." Almost as an afterthought, he added, "I hope it was because you care about me."

He took a deep breath. "And if you at least *care* about me, that could be a terrific start for us. I mean...if you were to stay here...we could try to make this marriage work. I know you're looking for the promise that you'll never be hurt." He shook his head dolefully. "I can't give you that. I love you, but I'm certain that if we are to spend our lives together, there will surely be arguments, there will surely be pain and sorrow. All I can promise is that I'll try my best to make you happy. I'll love you with all my heart."

"Stop it, Ben!" She jerked around, turning her back on him. Curling her fingers into a fist, she pressed it tight against her trembling lips. Couldn't he see how he was torturing her? Why was he doing this?

Yet, everything he'd said was true. Living without close emotional bonds *was* an empty shell of an existence. And she did care about him; she'd offered him all that she had because she cared so much.

But could she trust him with her heart?

He grasped her shoulders and she let him pull her to him. He pressed the length of his body against hers and his voice was thick with emotion as he whispered close to her ear, "As God is my witness, I do love you. I know you believe I'm only saying this because of the baby." He hesitated. "I do love the baby, Chels. I do. I want to be his father. I want to watch him grow up. I want to wipe his runny nose and kiss his bruised knees. I want to teach him how to drive a tractor. Plant a tree. I want it all."

His words became shaky. "I have to be honest with you and tell you that I do love our baby. But—"

He turned her around to face him and cradled her cheeks between his hands.

"I loved you first."

Chelsea felt her eyes fill with tears. Those were the words she'd longed to hear all her life. Could she believe he meant what he said?

Looking into his candid green eyes, she realized that Ben had just given to her what she had refused all along to give to him. He had trusted her enough to reveal what was in his heart. Without knowing what she would say or how she would react, Ben had exposed his emotions to her. He'd made himself vulnerable.

She knew then that he meant the words he'd said. She knew that it had been his feelings for her—not their baby—that had made him say them. She had so much she wanted to tell him, so many emotions she wanted to express, she only hoped she was able to speak around the huge lump that had formed in her throat.

"Oh, Ben," she was finally able to say, "there aren't words to express how much I love you."

When she saw the genuine relief that melted his gaze, Chelsea felt the weight of all her negative emotions lift from her. She felt light and carefree as joy filled her.

Ben loved her. Ben loved her!

He covered her mouth with his and kissed her deeply, thoroughly. And when he ended his kiss, his hand moved to the intimate spot on her lower belly where their child was nestled.

"We'll be a family," he said.

Chelsea smiled broadly, her happiness overflowing in the single tear that slid down her cheek.

"Let's go tell Aunt May," he suggested.

She nodded and felt as if she were floating through the grove of apple trees and into the country store.

The store was empty, but the two of them heard the loud, labored *tap, tap, tap,* as someone used the old hunt-and-peck method on the keys of the ancient manual typewriter in Chelsea's office.

"Do you think that's May?" There was bewilderment in Ben's question. "What could she be doing?"

"I don't know," Chelsea said.

They entered the office just in time to see May zip the paper from the old typewriter's roller with one smooth pull.

When the older woman turned and saw the two of them, she remarked, "Well, I see you've got yourselves all straightened out."

Chelsea knew the euphoric expressions on their faces told May all she needed to know.

"What are you up to?" Ben asked his aunt.

"See for yourself." She proudly handed the neatly typed paper to Ben.

"Elvis Is Alive and Well in Acapulco," Ben read the title aloud. His mouth split into a grin. "Why, it's an article for the tabloid. Are you going to submit it?"

May nodded proudly.

"I didn't know you'd been to Acapulco, May," Chelsea said.

"She hasn't," Ben commented wryly.

May cocked an eyebrow and haughtily snatched the article from her grandnephew. "Someone once told me that you shouldn't believe *everything* you read." She sauntered from the office as though she'd just put him in his place.

When Chelsea and Ben's laughter subsided, Ben wrapped her in his strong, protective arms. She felt all warm and fuzzy inside, and marveled at how their baby was snuggled between them.

This baby had been her dream. The one thing she'd thought would fulfill all her hopes of a happy future. But now, looking into the eyes of the man who loved her, she understood just how happy her future would be. With Ben by her side, she knew she could face the memories of yesterday and the unknown of tomorrow.

Slipping her hand through Ben's hair, she pulled him closer. She placed her lips on his in a long, lingering kiss and knew for certain that *all* her dreams were coming true.

Epilogue

Taking full advantage of the afternoon sunshine, Chelsea pushed the big-wheeled carriage over the uneven ground of the orchard. The warmth and freshness of spring was in the air, and she couldn't help but smile as she inhaled the delicious fragrance of the blossoming apple trees that surrounded her and her beautiful baby daughter.

As she neared the crew of working men, Chelsea sought and found the broad shoulders belonging to her husband. Ben's sinewy back muscles bunched, relaxed, then bunched again under the thin material of his cotton work shirt, and Chelsea felt a flame of desire flare in the pit of her belly. She was amazed how, even after nearly a year of marriage, the fiery passion she felt still blazed white-hot at the mere sight of him.

One of the employees must have alerted Ben to her arrival, for he turned toward her, his face conveying his pleasant surprise when his gaze locked on her. He hurried toward her, tugging off his work gloves and tucking them into his back pocket.

"Hi," he said, then tipped up her chin with his fingers and kissed her full on the mouth.

The feel of his warm, firm lips on her own made her heart lurch with overwhelming love. He pulled back and smiled.

"Hi, yourself," she whispered. "Kelly and I thought we'd come and visit Daddy."

Ben bent over the carriage. "So, my ladies came to see me." He reached in and gingerly scooped up the precious bundle.

Chelsea watched him cradle their baby in the crook of his arm and run a gentle finger over the velvety softness of her cheek. Seeing father and daughter together filled her with blissful contentment.

The baby cooed and Ben's fascinated gaze never left Kelly's face as he remarked, "She's smiling at me."

"I know," Chelsea said. Then she wryly added, "Although Aunt May keeps insisting it's only gas."

"May's become extremely opinionated these days." Ben's face took on a long-suffering expression.

Chelsea had to chuckle. "You *do* have to admit, her personal column in the local paper is a huge success."

"Yes, but does that success have to go to her head?" Ben laughed, then grew quiet as he gazed lovingly at his baby girl. "She's inherited my mother's dimple." There was awe in his voice and he tenderly caressed the tiny indentation in Kelly's cheek.

Chelsea took a moment to look around her. "The trees are beautiful this year."

Ben nodded. "I've never seen so many blooms," he told her. "If God's willing, we'll have an excellent harvest this fall. One that will go a long way in making up for last year's loss."

His intense green eyes were like a powerful magnet that drew Chelsea's gaze.

"Your money saved us this winter," he said. "I didn't have to lay off the men or—"

"*Our* money," she gently corrected him.

He reached out and ran his fingertips along her jaw. "I'm a lucky man."

Reaching up, Chelsea cupped her hand over his and pressed his work-roughened palm to her cheek.

"I'm the lucky one."

Ben pulled her to him and she snuggled against his chest next to their baby. The aroma of apple blossoms and baby powder wafted around them. Then another fragrance overtook her senses—a familiar male scent that impelled her to reach on tiptoe and press her nose to the heated skin of Ben's neck. She planted a kiss there and was delighted to feel his pulse quicken against her lips.

"Tonight." She whispered the promise in his ear and saw his mouth pull into a sensuous, knowing grin.

The aura of love that surrounded the three of them was strong, stable and secure. Chelsea watched Ben tuck Kelly into the padded carriage and marveled at the warm sentiment coursing through her.

Entrusting Ben with all her honest, open emotions had been the hardest, yet the most wonderful decision she'd ever made. All the years she'd spent distancing herself from others had been a terrible, lonely mistake. She reached out and touched his silky, sunbleached hair and was rewarded with his smile. He took hold of her hand and entwined his fingers with hers.

The heavy burden she carried from her past had somehow lightened over the months simply by revealing her bad memories to the man who loved and cared for her. Slowly, but surely, Ben was helping her to understand that she couldn't possibly hold herself responsible for the awful things that had happened to her as a child. Releasing the anger she felt toward her mother and other people from her past was a tedious but necessary and healthy process.

The close, intimate relationship she and Ben had developed over the past year continued to bring her unspeakable joy. Standing in the middle of the apple orchard with the man of her dreams and the beautiful baby they had created, Chelsea understood she couldn't know what the future held for them, but she did realize that, with Ben by her side, she could face the memories of yesterday and the unknown of tomorrow.

*   *   *   *   *

Silhouette ROMANCE™

COMING NEXT MONTH

#1042 A FATHER BETRAYED—Val Whisenand
Fabulous Fathers
Was Sami Adamson's child really his own? Clay Ellis didn't know—but he refused to believe the woman he'd always loved would keep him from the son he'd always wanted....

#1043 LONG LOST HUSBAND—Joleen Daniels
Andrea Ballanger thought her ex-husband, Travis Hunter, had been killed in the line of duty. But when she learned Travis was very much alive, she discovered her love was, too....

#1044 HARDHEADED WOMAN—Terry Essig
Divorce did wonders for Claire Martinson. Now that she had her independence, she was determined to be a new woman. But how was G. T. Greer going to convince her he'd fallen for the girl she'd always been?

#1045 BACHELOR AT THE WEDDING—Sandra Steffen
Wedding Wager
When confirmed bachelor Kyle Harris caught the wedding garter, he was surprisingly happy with the consequences. Now he just had to convince would-be bride Clarissa Cohagan that *he* was the man for *her*....

#1046 THE BABY WISH—Myrna Mackenzie
Gabriel Bonner was shocked when his pretty housekeeper, Maureen O'Shay, asked him to father her child. Worse still, now he was falling in love with her! What was a man who'd given up on family life to do?

#1047 HOME TIES—Kara Larkin
Sterling, Montana, needed a doctor and Dr. Bryant Conover needed a place to spend time with his son. He never expected to fall for Deborah Pingree. Suddenly making house calls was *very* appealing....

MILLION DOLLAR SWEEPSTAKES (III)

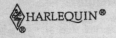 HARLEQUIN®  Silhouette®

The movie event of the season can be the reading event of the year!

Lights... The lights go on in October when CBS presents Harlequin/Silhouette Sunday Matinee Movies. These four movies are based on bestselling Harlequin and Silhouette novels.

Camera... As the cameras roll, be the first to read the original novels the movies are based on!

Action... Through this offer, you can have these books sent directly to you! Just fill in the order form below and you could be reading the books...before the movie!

48288-4	Treacherous Beauties by Cheryl Emerson $3.99 U.S./$4.50 CAN.	☐
83305-9	Fantasy Man by Sharon Green $3.99 U.S./$4.50 CAN.	☐
48289-2	A Change of Place by Tracy Sinclair $3.99 U.S./$4.50CAN.	☐
83306-7	Another Woman by Margot Dalton $3.99 U.S./$4.50 CAN.	☐

TOTAL AMOUNT	$
POSTAGE & HANDLING	$
($1.00 for one book, 50¢ for each additional)	
APPLICABLE TAXES*	$ _____
TOTAL PAYABLE	$ _____
(check or money order—please do not send cash)	

To order, complete this form and send it, along with a check or money order for the total above, payable to Harlequin Books, to: **In the U.S.:** 3010 Walden Avenue, P.O. Box 9047, Buffalo, NY 14269-9047; **In Canada:** P.O. Box 613, Fort Erie, Ontario, L2A 5X3.

Name: _____

Address: _____ City: _____

State/Prov.: _____ Zip/Postal Code: _____

*New York residents remit applicable sales taxes.
 Canadian residents remit applicable GST and provincial taxes.

CBSPR

"HOORAY FOR HOLLYWOOD" SWEEPSTAKES

HERE'S HOW THE SWEEPSTAKES WORKS

OFFICIAL RULES — NO PURCHASE NECESSARY

To enter, complete an Official Entry Form or hand print on a 3" x 5" card the words "HOORAY FOR HOLLYWOOD", your name and address and mail your entry in the pre-addressed envelope (if provided) or to: "Hooray for Hollywood" Sweepstakes, P.O. Box 9076, Buffalo, NY 14269-9076 or "Hooray for Hollywood" Sweepstakes, P.O. Box 637, Fort Erie, Ontario L2A 5X3. Entries must be sent via First Class Mail and be received no later than 12/31/94. No liability is assumed for lost, late or misdirected mail.

Winners will be selected in random drawings to be conducted no later than January 31, 1995 from all eligible entries received.

Grand Prize: A 7-day/6-night trip for 2 to Los Angeles, CA including round trip air transportation from commercial airport nearest winner's residence, accommodations at the Regent Beverly Wilshire Hotel, free rental car, and $1,000 spending money. (Approximate prize value which will vary dependent upon winner's residence: $5,400.00 U.S.); 500 Second Prizes: A pair of "Hollywood Star" sunglasses (prize value: $9.95 U.S. each). Winner selection is under the supervision of D.L. Blair, Inc., an independent judging organization, whose decisions are final. Grand Prize travelers must sign and return a release of liability prior to traveling. Trip must be taken by 2/1/96 and is subject to airline schedules and accommodations availability.

Sweepstakes offer is open to residents of the U.S. (except Puerto Rico) and Canada who are 18 years of age or older, except employees and immediate family members of Harlequin Enterprises, Ltd., its affiliates, subsidiaries, and all agencies, entities or persons connected with the use, marketing or conduct of this sweepstakes. All federal, state, provincial, municipal and local laws apply. Offer void wherever prohibited by law. Taxes and/or duties are the sole responsibility of the winners. Any litigation within the province of Quebec respecting the conduct and awarding of prizes may be submitted to the Regie des loteries et courses du Quebec. All prizes will be awarded; winners will be notified by mail. No substitution of prizes are permitted. Odds of winning are dependent upon the number of eligible entries received.

Potential grand prize winner must sign and return an Affidavit of Eligibility within 30 days of notification. In the event of non-compliance within this time period, prize may be awarded to an alternate winner. Prize notification returned as undeliverable may result in the awarding of prize to an alternate winner. By acceptance of their prize, winners consent to use of their names, photographs, or likenesses for purpose of advertising, trade and promotion on behalf of Harlequin Enterprises, Ltd., without further compensation unless prohibited by law. A Canadian winner must correctly answer an arithmetical skill-testing question in order to be awarded the prize.

For a list of winners (available after 2/28/95), send a separate stamped, self-addressed envelope to: Hooray for Hollywood Sweepstakes 3252 Winners, P.O. Box 4200, Blair, NE 68009.

CBSRLS

┌─────────────────────────────────────┐
│ **OFFICIAL ENTRY COUPON**   │
└─────────────────────────────────────┘

"Hooray for Hollywood"
SWEEPSTAKES!

Yes, I'd love to win the Grand Prize — a vacation in Hollywood —
or one of 500 pairs of "sunglasses of the stars"! Please enter me
in the sweepstakes!

This entry must be received by December 31, 1994.
Winners will be notified by January 31, 1995.

Name _____

Address _____ Apt. _____

City _____

State/Prov. _____ Zip/Postal Code _____

Daytime phone number _____
(area code)

Mail all entries to: Hooray for Hollywood Sweepstakes,
P.O. Box 9076, Buffalo, NY 14269-9076.
In Canada, mail to: Hooray for Hollywood Sweepstakes,
P.O. Box 637, Fort Erie, ON L2A 5X3.

KCH

┌─────────────────────────────────────┐
│ **OFFICIAL ENTRY COUPON**   │
└─────────────────────────────────────┘

"Hooray for Hollywood"
SWEEPSTAKES!

Yes, I'd love to win the Grand Prize — a vacation in Hollywood —
or one of 500 pairs of "sunglasses of the stars"! Please enter me
in the sweepstakes!

This entry must be received by December 31, 1994.
Winners will be notified by January 31, 1995.

Name _____

Address _____ Apt. _____

City _____

State/Prov. _____ Zip/Postal Code _____

Daytime phone number _____
(area code)

Mail all entries to: Hooray for Hollywood Sweepstakes,
P.O. Box 9076, Buffalo, NY 14269-9076.
In Canada, mail to: Hooray for Hollywood Sweepstakes,
P.O. Box 637, Fort Erie, ON L2A 5X3.

KCH